Who said she wanted to get married, anyhow?

Bridget thought as she pulled away from the ranch house.

Who would want a ready-made family? Who would want to spend their life in some small town?

She bit her lip to keep from calling out the answer.

She would.

Wistfully, she glanced in the rearview mirror. And suddenly there Josh was, galloping toward her on a wild mustang. If she was smart she would have put her car in gear and driven away as fast as she could, but now it was too late. Closer and closer he came until he filled her mirror, her mind and her thoughts.

As he pulled the horse up beside her car, she wondered for the hundredth time what made her heart thud wildly every time she saw him.

He was handsome. He was rugged. He was sexy.

But it was more than that.

So much more.

Dear Reader,

Traditionally June is the month for weddings, so Silhouette Romance cordially invites you to enjoy our promotion JUNE BRIDES, starting with Suzanne Carey's *Sweet Bride of Revenge.* In this sensuously powerful VIRGIN BRIDES tale, a man forces the daughter of his nemesis to marry him, never counting on falling in love with the enemy....

Up-and-comer Robin Nicholas delivers a touching BUNDLES OF JOY titled *Man, Wife and Little Wonder.* Can a denim-clad, Harley-riding bad boy turn doting dad and dedicated husband? Find out in this classic marriage-of-convenience romance! Next, Donna Clayton's delightful duo MOTHER & CHILD continues with the evocative title *Who's the Father of Jenny's Baby?* A woman awakens in the hospital to discover she has amnesia—and she's pregnant! Problem is, *two* men claim to be the baby's father—her estranged husband...and her husband's brother!

Granted: Wild West Bride is the next installment in Carol Grace's BEST-KEPT WISHES series. This richly Western romance pairs a toughened, taut-muscled cowboy and a sophisticated city gal who welcomes his kisses, but will she accept his ring? For a fresh spin on the bridal theme, try Alice Sharpe's *Wife on His Doorstep.* An about-to-be bride stops her wedding to the wrong man, only to land on the doorstep of the strong, silent ship captain who was to perform the ill-fated nuptials.... And in Leanna Wilson's latest Romance, *His Tomboy Bride,* Nick Latham was *supposed* to "give away" childhood friend and bride-to-be Billie Rae—not claim the transformed beauty as his own!

We hope you enjoy the month's wedding fun, and return each and every month for more classic, emotional, heartwarming novels from Silhouette Romance.

Enjoy!

Joan Marlow Golan

Joan Marlow Golan
Senior Editor Silhouette Romance

Please address questions and book requests to:
Silhouette Reader Service
U.S.: 3010 Walden Ave., P.O. Box 1325, Buffalo, NY 14269
Canadian: P.O. Box 609, Fort Erie, Ont. L2A 5X3

GRANTED: WILD WEST BRIDE

Carol Grace

Silhouette
R O M A N C E™
Published by Silhouette Books
America's Publisher of Contemporary Romance

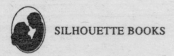

SILHOUETTE BOOKS

ISBN 0-373-19303-3

GRANTED: WILD WEST BRIDE

Copyright © 1998 by Carol Culver

This edition published by arrangement with Harlequin Books S.A.

® and TM are trademarks of Harlequin Books S.A., used under license. Trademarks indicated with ® are registered in the United States Patent and Trademark Office, the Canadian Trade Marks Office and in other countries.

Printed in U.S.A.

Books by Carol Grace

Silhouette Romance

Make Room for Nanny #690
A Taste of Heaven #751
Home Is Where the Heart Is #882
Mail-Order Male #955
The Lady Wore Spurs #1010
*Lonely Millionaire #1057
*Almost A Husband #1105
*Almost Married #1142
The Rancher and the Lost Bride #1153
†Granted: Big Sky Groom #1277
†Granted: Wild West Bride #1303

*Miramar Inn
†Best-Kept Wishes

Silhouette Desire

Wife for a Night #1118
The Heiress Inherits a Cowboy #1145

CAROL GRACE

has always been interested in travel and living abroad.
She spent her junior year in college in France and toured
the world working on the hospital ship *Hope*. She and
her husband spent the first year and a half of their marriage in Iran, where they both taught English. Then, with
their toddler daughter, they lived in Algeria for
two years.

Carol says that writing is another way of making her life
exciting. Her office is her mountaintop home, which
overlooks the Pacific Ocean and which she shares with
her inventor husband, their daughter, who is now
twenty-one years old and a senior in college, and their
seventeen-year-old son.

Cowboy Josh Gentry's Wish List

1. To raise Max, my hell-raiser five-year-old son, as best I can by myself.

2. To keep my mind on taming wild mustangs, and not get distracted by Bridget McCloud, the advertising executive with all kinds of crazy plans for me.

3. To avoid falling in love again——especially with Bridget, who doesn't belong here in wild mustang country.

4. To get Bridget off my ranch before I find myself wishing this big-city beauty would turn into a Wild West bride....

Chapter One

Bridget McCloud braced her elbows against the wooden fence and held her binoculars up to her eyes. There on a hilltop, riding a wild mustang horse, was the man she was looking for—strong, virile, powerful and sexy. Unable to restrain herself, she let out a whoop of joy. She was not a bounty hunter or a desperate spinster. She was the president and owner of Bridget McCloud Advertising, about to land her first major account with the manufacturers of Wild Mustang men's cologne.

Now that she'd found her Wild Mustang Man, nothing could stop her. She grinned to herself, wishing her administrative assistant and best friend Kate was there to share the excitement and the view. Not that she would have surrendered her binoculars. Not just yet.

Silhouetted against the blue Nevada sky, wild horse and rider moved as one. Bridget could almost hear the rhythmic fall of the hoofbeats, feel the muscles ripple under the man's denim shirt and smell...yes, she could almost smell the tangy, masculine scent of Wild Mustang men's cologne.

With a sigh of ecstasy, she let the binoculars fall against her chest and grabbed her camera from its case to snap a whole roll of pictures. She never saw the bicycle bearing down on her from out of nowhere. If she had she would have leaped out of the way before it plowed into her and knocked her to the ground.

The bike crashed onto the dirt road, the rider thrown to the side. Bridget staggered to her feet, dazed and bruised, head pounding. The daredevil rider, all four feet of him, was sitting in the dirt, staring at his skinned knees.

"Sorry," he said, wide blue eyes looking up at her as she limped toward him. "Didn't know anybody was there."

"Same here," she acknowledged. "But I think you got the worst of it. You or your bike," she said, noticing the smashed spokes, the twisted handlebars. "I better take you home and get you bandaged up."

"I *am* home," he said, waving at the fields on the other side of the fence. Painfully he got to his feet, but his knees buckled and Bridget caught him in her arms before he lost his balance again. His dusty hair tickled her nose. She felt his body stiffen like a wounded animal, before he yanked himself out of her arms. "I'm okay," he said, his upper lip stiff with pride. But his voice shook ever so slightly. "I can crawl through the fence and be back before my dad knows I'm gone."

Bridget frowned at his stubborn determination, more than a little concerned about the cut above his eye and the blood oozing from his knees.

"What if I crawl through the fence with you and make sure you get there?" she offered.

He shrugged his narrow shoulders, and his teeth chattered. Bridget wondered if there were more injuries than met the eye or if he was that afraid of his father. "Okay, but we gotta hurry. If my dad finds out about this he'll have my hide.''

"What's left of it," Bridget muttered, giving him a worried glance as she followed him, squeezing herself through the slats in the fence.

The two of them staggered up a sagebrush-covered hill toward a sprawling ranch house, two steps forward, one step back as Bridget's binoculars bounced against her chest, and her camera case swung back and forth from her shoulder. She began to wonder who was helping whom. The further they walked, the stronger the boy got, and the weaker Bridget felt. Oh, to be young again, she thought, as he pulled her forward, his small grubby hand in hers. Oh, to be wearing sensible shoes instead of sandals.

She wasn't married, though she'd always thought she would be by now, and imagined the little hand tucked in hers as the hand of her own child. She sighed. Because it was not to be. She'd seen her plans for marriage and a family go down the drain this past year and was proceeding full steam ahead on the next best thing—her career. She couldn't deny, however, that the stubby little hand in hers brought a rush of maternal and protective feelings she thought she'd successfully buried, even though she, with her bruises, was in no shape to protect anyone, especially not this tough little kid here.

"How old are you?" Bridget gasped, the hot dry air searing her lungs as she trudged slowly upward.

"Five and a half. Going on six." He turned to look up at her, squinting in the bright sunlight. "How 'bout you?"

"Thirty-one."

His blue eyes widened in amazement. "You don't look that old."

"Thank you," Bridget said with a reluctant smile.

"My dad's older than you."

"Really? Is he around, by any chance?"

The boy pointed to the hill behind the house. "Out riding."

"What about your mom?"

He pointed up at the cloudless blue sky. "She's in heaven."

Bridget was stunned into momentary silence and her leaden feet stopped moving.

"Come on," he urged, almost jerking her arm out of its socket.

She picked up her feet, wiped the perspiration off her forehead and forced herself to move. This was no time for gratuitous sympathy. Besides, she had no idea what to say to a boy whose mom is in heaven. This was a time to change the subject.

"Does your dad ride wild mustangs?" she asked, pausing to catch her breath.

"How'd you know?"

"If his name is Gentry, I've heard about him. That's why I'm here. I want to talk to him."

"'Bout a horse?"

Bridget refrained from saying, No, it's 'bout a men's cologne. This wasn't the time or place to broach the subject of his father as a male model, so she just nodded. And thanked God the large, stone ranch house was now only steps away.

As the boy pushed the heavy, oak front door open, Bridget drew a deep breath and stepped into the quintessential Western living room with native rugs on the wide-planked floors and large leather chairs flanking a huge stone fireplace. Their footsteps echoed off the thick walls of the empty house.

She had a brief, fleeting view of a large, framed photograph of a woman on top of the mantel before the boy dragged her down a long hallway to a cool, tiled bathroom. Before she could stop him, he was kneeling on the sink, dripping blood all over the aqua porcelain and pawing frantically through the medicine chest, tossing bottles and jars and tubes to the floor where they landed in noisy confusion.

"Stop, whatever your name is, and let me clean you up," Bridget demanded, setting her equipment on the edge of the tub. With a burst of energy, she lifted the boy off the sink, sat him firmly on the toilet seat and grabbed a washcloth from a towel rack. Miraculously he held still, hands clenched into fists, his face pale under a smattering of freckles while she carefully cleaned the wounds on his knees with soap and water then turned her attention to the laceration over his eye.

Boys, she thought with a flash of intuition—this is what they do. They fall off their bikes. They skin their knees. And this is what their moms do. They clean them up. But she was not his mom. She was nobody's mom. And wasn't likely to ever be. Not the way her life was going. That was okay. There were other things to do besides being a mother. And she was doing them. But for the first time in weeks the face of Scott Marsten flashed before her eyes. His cruel words rang in her ears.

"Face it, Bridget, you just don't have what it takes to make a man happy. I thought it was because you put all your effort into your job, but now it turns out you haven't got what it takes to make it in advertising, either."

Blinking back a sudden rush of tears, Bridget peeled the adhesive off an extra-large-size Band-Aid when heavy footsteps resounded down the hall, and a loud, angry voice called, "Max, where are you?"

So that was his name. Max froze, his eyes wide with fright. Bridget slapped the bandage on the boy's knee while she imagined an angry Paul Bunyon on his way to skin *both* their hides with his ax.

"What in the hell is going on here?" the man demanded,

filling the doorway with his six-foot, three-inch frame, and pinning Bridget with his piercing blue eyes.

"It…it was an accident," she stuttered, suddenly feeling five and a half, going on six, instead of a mature thirty-one, going on thirty-two.

His gaze shifted to his son, who was now standing, feet planted apart, staring up at his father. "Max?"

"I ran into this lady on my bike, and I gotta go get it. She came to see you 'bout a horse," he said edging around his father. Bridget's wobbly legs wouldn't hold her up another minute. She sank to the commode as she listened to Max's footsteps racing back down the hall. When the front door slammed shut, she looked up into stormy blue eyes under a furrowed wide brow.

"I can explain," she said weakly. This was not how she planned to meet the man destined to sell a million bottles of men's cologne in the next year. Not sitting on a toilet seat with her leg gashed in six places, her forehead pounding, one eye almost swollen shut. But now that he was standing only a few feet away, she was more convinced than ever that he was the one. On his horse he was a magnificent figure of a man. Off his horse, he was…he was everything she'd ever dreamed of. For her men's cologne campaign, of course. Tough, handsome, rugged, sexy— Suddenly she felt faint. She leaned forward and put her head between her knees.

"What's wrong?" Leaning forward too, Josh Gentry braced his hands on her shoulders and lifted her head to face him. He'd been so worried about Max he hadn't noticed the woman's eye was black-and-blue and almost completely closed. Not only that but one leg was gashed in several places.

"Good God, you're hurt. Did Max do this?"

She shook her head, which didn't make it feel any better.

"It was nobody's fault. I was just in the wrong place at the wrong time."

Josh grabbed a clean towel from the shelf, doused it with soap and water and gently cleaned the dirt from her wounds. He'd done it many times for horses, and often for Max, but never for a woman with spectacular legs in linen shorts. It had been so long since he'd noticed a woman's legs or anything at all about them, he felt slightly dazed himself, as if he was the one who'd been run down by a bicycle.

"I'm sorry about this," he said, applying antiseptic cream and bandages, then helping her to her feet. "Where did you say it happened?"

She pointed in a general westerly direction. "On the dirt road, just outside your fence."

He nodded, clamping his lips together to keep from exploding. Max was supposed to be at his grandparents' ranch today, learning to groom horses. "Let's get some ice for your eye," he said grimly.

"I'm fine, really," she protested, grabbing her camera case and binoculars before he walked her down the hall toward the kitchen, holding tightly to her arm in case she decided to bolt and then sue him later for negligence. She was gutsy, he'd give her that. She hadn't even winced when he'd washed her wounds, and didn't complain about her eye. On the other hand, she was a city woman no doubt, from her clothes and her manner, a tourist taking pictures, one who might walk out of here saying she was okay and then fall apart and have hysterics.

A vision of his late wife, Molly, drifted before his eyes. Calm, serene and capable in the face of emergency, be it a crop failure or an accident in the field or feeding twenty-five hungry men on a moment's notice. If she were here, she'd have the woman wrapped in a quilt on the couch, treating her with an ice pack and some hot soup. The quintessential nurturer. So good at coping with emergencies he almost thought she went out looking for them. So busy taking care of everybody else, she didn't seem to have time for him.

He forced those traitorous thoughts from his mind. Molly was a saint. Everyone said so. They said so even before she died from a deadly virus two years ago. Certainly his life had never been the same since. And never would be again. Just thinking of how his plans for the perfect life with the perfect wife had gone so wrong left a bitter taste in his mouth.

He reached into the freezer and grabbed a handful of ice cubes, put them in a plastic bag and pressed it against the woman's eyelid, holding it tightly for her as she sat at his kitchen table.

"How does that feel?" he asked.

"Fine," she said, taking the ice bag from him and laying it on the table instead of against her eye. She was lying. She was too pale to be fine, but her smile was more determined than sincere.

"I'm Bridget McCloud," she said extending her hand. "McCloud Advertising." Automatically he took her hand and was struck by her firm grip. A woman used to getting what she wanted, he guessed.

It didn't take long to find out what she wanted. Him.

"I'm in your area today looking for someone to represent my client, the makers of Wild Mustang cologne."

Forgetting the ice pack now leaking onto the round oak table, Josh straddled a straight-back chair across from the woman and stared at her. "You're making a cologne that smells like wild mustangs?" he asked.

A tinge of color came back to her cheeks. "Obviously it won't smell exactly like horses. What they've done is to capture the essence of the wild mustang. You know, leather and…and—"

"Manure?" he asked.

She pursed her lips together, obviously annoyed with him. "Of course not. Putting the scent aside—"

"The *smell*, you mean," he said, almost enjoying tweaking her like this. She was so damned citified, so proper, so businesslike. And way off base.

"Whatever. That aside, the purpose of my visit today—"

"Besides being run over and getting banged up," he filled in. "By the way, what were you doing standing outside my fence?"

"Looking for the Wild Mustang Man. Looking for you." Her one hazel eye that wasn't closed shut gleamed with excitement.

"And taking pictures...of me?"

"Yes, you. I've come all the way up here from San Francisco to look for a man who embodies all the qualities of the Wild West. When I saw you on your horse up there on the hill, I knew I'd found him."

"But I don't wear cologne. I don't know anyone who does. I wouldn't want to know anyone who does. So that lets me out."

She leaned forward, elbows on the table. "Not at all. You don't have to wear cologne. You don't have to wear anything." Her eyes traveled over his dusty denim shirt and his faded Levi's and she blushed. Hastily she brought her gaze back to his. "I mean, just clothes, of course—a checkered shirt, along with the vest, the chaps, the scarf. For the color print ads and the TV commercials. I can see it now."

He jumped to his feet. "Well, I can't. You've got the wrong man. You don't really think I'd make a fool of myself on TV, do you? Advertising some damned flaky perfume? God, I'd be the laughing stock of the whole town." The thought of men wearing perfume made him gag.

"Oh, come now," she said, standing to look him in the eye. "You're exaggerating."

"You think so?" he asked, glaring at her. "I've lived in Harmony all my life. You've been here, what, one day? My parents worked this land before me and their parents before them. We buy wild horses. We raise them and train them. And then we sell them. We *don't* wear perfume."

"Cologne," she corrected.

"And we don't pose for ads. We run a business."

"I understand that," she said. "I run a business too. The advertising business. My job is to find the perfect Wild Mustang Man. And now that I've found him I'm not going to let him go. Just because you pose on your horse for a few pictures doesn't mean you can't continue your own work. The crew will film you as you're doing your buying, selling, training...whatever you do. And you'll make enough money to send your son to college. You'll make more money than you've ever dreamed of."

"How do you know what I've dreamed of?" he demanded.

"I don't. I'm just trying—"

"You're trying to bribe me. Well, I can't be bought. Nothing you can say will make me change my mind. And now if you're feeling well enough to travel, I'll see you out." Finally, an excuse to get her out of there.

Bridget blinked. Surprised at being turned down, he thought. It was time she learned to take no for an answer and look elsewhere for this Wild Mustang Man. With his hand gripping her arm, he ushered her and her equipment to the front door. She didn't exactly drag the heels of her strappy sandals, but she didn't pick them up very readily, either.

"There are other ranchers, you know," he said, hoping to ease her quickly and smoothly out of his house. "Maybe you can convince one of them to sell his soul and make a fool of himself on TV. If you'd like some names—"

"I have plenty of names, thank you," she said stiffly,

holding tightly to the front doorknob. "But I know what I want."

"So do I," he said. "What I want is to be left alone by city slickers combing the countryside for male models."

"I'm not looking for a male model. If I was I could have found one in the city. I want a real man. With real muscles. A man who does real work. I want you. When you come to your senses, give me a call. I'm renting a room in town." She pulled her arm away, fished in her pocket for a card and thrust it at him.

"Don't hold your breath," he said. He took her card, intending to throw it away as soon as she was out of sight. It smelled like her, an expensive smell like hothouse flowers, and the sooner he got rid of her card and her *scent* the better. With relief he watched from the front step as she limped down his path and veered off through the field toward the road. With relief and just a touch of guilt. Maybe she was really hurt. And too proud to show it. He could have walked her to her car. It wouldn't have killed him. But all he'd done was to bandage her leg after his son had knocked her down and injured her.

His son. What was he going to do with Max? What was he going to do with his life? He buried his face in his hands. He wasn't cut out to be a single parent. He wasn't cut out to be single. At high school graduation he'd made a wish— to marry the only girl he'd ever loved and ever would love. He got his wish. He'd loved her, as best he could. And he'd married her, too soon maybe. Too young perhaps. And now what? Was he supposed to spend the rest of his life alone? Of course he was. That's what Molly would have done if he'd died first. But Molly was a saint. And he...he was a man, an ordinary man, with ordinary wants and needs. He crumpled her card in his hand, but instead of throwing it away, he stuffed it into his back pocket.

* * *

Bridget drove back to town, her head throbbing, her mind spinning and her leg aching. But undiscouraged. It took more than a refusal to discourage the daughter of Angus McCloud, the only Scotsman to run the San Francisco marathon at age eighty. He didn't win the marathon, but he finished it, as well as a bottle of Scotch whiskey at the celebration that followed. She parked in back of the diner on Main Street, glanced up at the second-floor room she was renting above the shoe repair shop, and decided to call her office from the pay phone before going up to shower and change her clothes.

"Kate," she said, when her friend answered. "You won't believe it, but I've found him. Honestly, in my wildest dreams, I couldn't have come up with a more perfect Wild Mustang Man."

"But you just got there."

"Isn't it amazing? My first day and I find a room to rent, I ask around, I get a list of ranchers and cowboys and the first one on my list, it's him."

"Him? Who?"

"Josh Gentry is his name. You'll love him, I guarantee it. The client will love him—"

"What about you, will you love him, too?" Kate asked worriedly. "Remember, Bridgie, you're in a very vulnerable state. You'll fall for the first man who smiles at you."

"Don't worry about that. This guy is not the smiley type," Bridget assured her, wishing her head wouldn't throb that way. Wishing she'd kept that ice on her eyelid. Wishing Kate would forget how Bridget had been dumped so Bridget could forget, too.

"You know I've learned my lesson," Bridget assured her. "In fact, I've learned so many lessons in the past year I can't keep them straight. Don't mix business and pleasure is one of them. Marriage and a family are not the only possibilities for women in this day and age."

"Don't fall in love with unavailable men is another," Kate reminded her. "And don't fall in love at first sight."

Bridget thought of the man who'd applied that washcloth to her shin, the man with the fierce gaze, the short temper and the gentle touch, and a shiver ran up her spine. "I won't. I'm going to devote myself to my work. I'm not going to fall in love at all. Never again," she said, gazing across Main Street to the vast high desert plains of Nevada, remembering the pain and the broken promises and the broken engagement.

"Never's a long time," Kate said.

"I can wait."

"Good girl. Now about the Wild Mustang Man. Should I call the client? Hire the crew? Buy some furniture for the office?"

"Maybe you'd better hold off for a few days," Bridget said. "There's just one little problem. The guy said no."

"No? He turned down a chance to be our Wild Mustang Man?" Kate asked incredulously.

"I think it was just the shock of…you know, the idea, the way I presented it, all at once. But he has my card, and once he's had a chance to think it over…well, he's probably trying to call me right now. And if he doesn't, I'll call him."

"We don't have a lot of time, Bridget. The rent on the office is due and I'm not sure we can stall any longer."

"Uh-oh. What I'd better do is send you the roll of film I just took. You can show the pictures to the Wild Mustang people. It will show them we're not just some little start-up with big ideas and nothing else. It will show them we're making progress. Maybe they'll even give us an advance."

"But what if they see the pictures, love the guy, give us an advance, and then he turns you down?"

"He's not going to turn me down," Bridget said with

more conviction than she felt. "Anyway, I have to go now and get some ice for my eye."

"What?"

"I was involved in a little accident on the road this morning."

"A traffic accident in Harmony, Nevada? I don't believe it."

"All kinds of things in Harmony you wouldn't believe," Bridget murmured.

Including a five-year-old boy who brought out the maternal feelings Bridget had determinedly squashed when her marriage plans went down the drain. A ranch house any woman would love, which had been carefully decorated by a woman who watched over it from her place on the mantel or somewhere in heaven.

That afternoon Josh called his parents from the phone in the kitchen to ask if they'd seen Max.

"Yep, he's here," his father said. "Came in draggin' his busted bike. Wants me to help him fix it."

"He's supposed to be helping you, not the other way around. Better send him home," Josh said.

"He's okay. In better shape than the woman he ran into, he says. Some woman looking for a horse?"

"Not exactly. She's looking for a *man* on a horse."

"She find him?"

"No," Josh said firmly

"Shouldn't have much trouble if she's as good-looking as Max says."

Josh shook his head. Had his five-year-old son noticed her tawny wheat gold hair that framed her face and the silky-smooth long legs? "That kid. I wish he'd show as much interest in horses as in ten-speed bikes."

"Or in pretty women," his father said with a chuckle. "Sure is nothing like you. All you ever cared about was the ranch and wild mustangs and the neighbor girl who turned into one pretty woman.''

"I haven't changed, Pop. That's all I'll ever care about. Now that Molly's gone I've still got the ranch and the horses, and Max, of course.''

"Since Molly's been gone for over two years, son, maybe it's time for you to move on.''

"I'm not going anywhere. You know that," Josh said. "This is my home and always will be. With or without Molly.''

"I don't mean geographically. I'm thinking of mentally. Molly would have—''

"Molly would have done the same. Stayed loyal to my memory.''

"Sure she would. Of course. But if she was here, and not you, I'd say the same thing. Get on with your life. Find someone to help you raise Max.''

"I've got you and Mom,'' Josh said.

"We're not going to be here forever," his father said.

"Where're you going?''

"No place. Not today. Not tomorrow. But someday…''

"We'll talk about it then," Josh said. "You know what I went through when Molly died. I'll never take another chance on love. Nothing is worth the pain I went through.''

"Stubborn. Well, that's one thing you and your son have in common.''

"You may have a point there. Just send him home when you get tired of him. Right now I've got a mare I've got to halter before I add another horse to my stable. If I can get to it without some damned woman coming around with a camera. You coming with me to the wild horse adoption center on Thursday?''

"Can't do it. Your mother's got me signed up for some volunteer work at the church.''

"And you want me to saddle myself to a woman again?''

"Now wait a minute," his father said.

"Can't wait. Got work to do."

When Max came home at the end of the day, with his repaired bicycle in the back of his grandfather's pickup, Josh sat down at the dinner table to have a talk with him.

"When I send you to your grandparents' house I expect you to stay there."

"I know," Max said, shoveling a mouthful of canned spaghetti into his mouth.

Josh closed his eyes for a moment, hoping that Molly didn't know he was feeding his son out of cans. At least he'd heated them tonight.

"If you'd been where you were supposed to be, doing what you were supposed to be doing, you wouldn't have run into the lady. And if you hadn't run into her, she wouldn't have come to our house and bothered me."

"Then who would have bandaged my knee?" Max asked with perfect five-year-old logic.

"You wouldn't— Never mind. I just want to know where you are."

"I'm right here, Dad."

"Yeah, I see you are." He dished out a bowl of spaghetti for himself. "Do you want me to pick out a burro for you at the sale this week? Or a pony?"

"Don't we got enough horses?" Max asked. "I rather have a motor bike."

Josh looked at his son with disbelief. If he hadn't personally been involved with the conception and the birth of this boy, he'd wonder if he could possibly be his. His father was right. At Max's age all he'd cared about was horses. Riding, training, grooming. He couldn't get enough. He even liked mucking out the stables. And his son wanted a motor bike!

Josh took a deep breath to keep from losing his cool. He glanced at the picture of a smiling Molly holding baby Max that was stuck to the refrigerator and grimaced. If she were here, she'd know what to say to him. But she wasn't. Josh was on his own.

All he could think of to say was the obvious. "You're too young for a motor bike."

His son frowned at him for a long moment, his mouth ringed with red tomato sauce, the black-and-blue bruise under his eye turning purple, still trying to figure out a way to get what he wanted. Finally Max finished his dinner and hopped off his chair. "What'd she say?" he asked.

"Who?" he asked, as if he didn't know.

"You know who," Max said.

"She said it wasn't your fault," Josh said.

Max grinned, showing spaces where his baby teeth were missing. "Didja like her?"

"No," Josh said. "But I can see you did."

Satisfied, Max darted out the back door to do wheelies on the front lawn on his newly repaired bike.

Josh stood at the window watching the little daredevil make ruts in the grass he'd so carefully seeded and watered. "I didn't like her," he repeated out loud. But he was no longer trying to convince his son, he was trying to convince himself.

Chapter Two

For two days Bridget combed the countryside in her old car, while her bruises healed and the swelling over her eye went down. She was looking for the Wild Mustang Man, but her heart wasn't in it, because she'd already found him. She knew it. Why didn't he know it, too?

Because he was stubborn, determined and opinionated. But so was she. And she was determined to get Josh Gentry. Just in case, though she owed it to the client to see what else was out there. So far what was out there was a seventy-eight-year-old cowboy named Slim, who'd been riding wild mustangs in competition for years. He was a nice guy, but he didn't have that...that...certain something that Josh had.

You couldn't really call it charm or charisma. You could call it sex appeal, she admitted reluctantly. But what was wrong with that? It was a known fact that more women bought cologne for men than men bought for themselves. And what sold products better than a sexy man? Nothing.

On the third day she stood in front of the café after a

large breakfast of biscuits and country gravy, studying a map of northern Nevada, wondering how long she could hold out. More to the point, how long her money would hold out. When she'd worked for Marsten and Grant Ad Agency and was on an expense account, she had blithely signed credit card receipts at the best restaurants and hotels on business trips.

No matter how much they paid her, Bridget wouldn't have gone back to the gigantic ad agency for anything. She'd only planned on working until she and Scott got married and started a family. Then she'd intended to give it all up. Happily. But everything changed when Scott broke up with her.

The company was just a small start-up ten years ago. Then, as they'd turned into a mega company, Scott, the vice president, got nervous and worried about the accounts. The result was the company stifled individual talent and lost their creative edge. The final straw for Bridget was when her erstwhile fiancé pulled an ad Bridget had written because it offended his boss.

Now that she had her own business, and every penny she spent had to be earned by herself, it was a different story. Until she landed a major account, she couldn't really afford to keep her office open, pay the rent and pay Kate's salary. Nor could she support herself on the road like this, though it was hard to imagine less expensive accommodations and cheaper meals than the ones she was getting in this small, dusty town.

She looked up and down the Main Street, as if she might find inspiration in the colorful Old-West storefronts, like the mock balcony painted on the second floor of the saloon, and she sighed.

She had to find her Wild Mustang Man. But how? Where? Should she return to the Gentry Ranch for one more try, and risk possible injury and certain rejection, or should she head out of town to the wild horse sale she'd heard mentioned as she was sipping her morning coffee in the diner? It had to be the perfect place to find a wild mustang man. If only she could push Josh Gentry out of her mind and give somebody else a chance.

Bridget glanced up as a station wagon pulled up in front of the general store across the street and a small boy and a gray-haired woman got out. The boy turned to look at her. When he recognized her he shouted a greeting so raucous two men lumbering through town in their tractor turned to look at her.

"Hello, Max," she called, crossing the street to see for herself how his wounds had healed. "How are you?"

"Okay," he said, bracing one small hand against the car. "My dad said you went home."

"Did he? No, I'm still here. That was just wishful thinking on his part."

"What's wishful thinking?"

"It's, uh…"

"I kinda thought you were still here. Didja get your horse yet?"

"No, not really."

"My grandma's taking care of me today," he said nodding in the direction of the pleasant-looking woman in tan slacks and a crisp white shirt. "'Cuz my dad's not home. That's the lady I was telling you about," he said to his grandmother. "The one who's looking for a horse."

"I'm Joan Gentry," said the woman, losing no time in extending her hand in a friendly manner. "So you're the poor woman Max ran over. I should have recognized you from his description."

Max's description, not Josh's, Bridget thought.

"I'm so sorry about the accident. I hope you're feeling better," the older woman continued.

"Oh, heavens, yes," Bridget said airily. "It was really

nothing at all. And just as much my fault as anyone's. I was standing there engrossed. That is, I was watching...*not* watching I mean, and not thinking.''

"I see," Joan Gentry said with a smile. "Nevertheless I want to apologize on behalf of Max. I hope your injuries haven't discouraged you from buying a wild mustang from my son.''

"Well, actually..." Bridget looked down at Max, then back up at his grandmother, noting that electric blue eyes ran in the family. How had this story about her wanting to buy a horse got started? She shifted from one brown loafer to another trying to decide whether to deny she was looking for a horse and confess she was looking for a man instead. A special man. Her son.

"We're goin' to the hardware store," Max said, tugging impatiently at his grandmother's hand. "Grandma's buying me a slingshot. Wanna come?"

Bridget hesitated only a second. If Josh Gentry wasn't home then there was no point going to his ranch. "No, I can't. I'm going to a wild horse sale."

"That's where my dad is," Max said.

"Really?" Bridget patted Max on the head affectionately. "That's great." It *was* great. She'd run into him "by accident," and if she didn't convince him to be her Wild Mustang Man today, then she'd find somebody else at that sale who would do. They wouldn't be the same, but they'd do.

"Yeah, he can help you pick one out. And train it for you," Max said.

"Good idea," she said. If she had to buy a horse to get the man interested, she'd do it. How expensive could a wild horse be, anyway?

"Do you ride a bicycle, too?" he asked.

"I don't really ride anything," she confessed. "Not yet."

"What about a slingshot?" he continued. "Know how to use one?"

"'Fraid not."

"You've got a lot to learn," Max observed.

"Max!" his grandmother.

Bridget smiled and ruffled the boy's taffy-colored hair. She wasn't offended. She *did* have a lot to learn. And most of it had nothing to do with bikes or horses or slingshots. It had to do with love and life. She sighed.

"Well, it was good seeing you Max. Nice to meet you, Mrs. Gentry."

As she drove down Main Street, she met her image in her rearview mirror and told herself sternly that if she couldn't convince Josh Gentry to be her Wild Mustang Man today, she didn't belong in the advertising business. But what would she use to convince him? She'd already tried money and fame. What did he want?

Some twenty miles out of town was the Bureau of Land Management's holding facility. After parking her car, Bridget made her way through the dusty parking lot where proud new owners were already loading their newly adopted animals into horse trailers. She heard snatches of conversation as she walked down the alley between rows of green-paneled corrals, covertly glancing from right to left at the men in broad-brimmed hats, looking...wondering if one of them would do, as their conversation swirled around her.

"Not that one. She looks like a rocking horse."

"Ya paid too much."

"Call that a horse?"

"I wanted the bay but she's come up lame."

"Ask Gentry. He knows horses."

"Ain't seen him."

"He's here."

He'd better be there, Bridget thought. Because so far she

hadn't seen anyone who could hold a candle to him. Since she'd first seen him the other day, she hadn't been able to shake the image of him as her Wild Mustang Man. Face it, she just plain hadn't been able to shake his image, period. Was it just the contrast between him and the city men she was used to, who paled by comparison? Or was it just that he was the first honest-to-goodness rancher she'd ever seen and his rugged image was indelibly engraved on her subconscious?

As she rounded the corner of the stucco county building, Bridget was struck by the sound of braying burros and the sight of about 150 wild horses milling nervously in holding pens, upset by the presence of the humans who'd come to look them over and possibly buy them and take them home.

With her ever-present camera hanging around her neck, she stopped at the metal fence and snapped a few pictures of the animals, once running wild and free in the Nevada desert, now trapped behind metal bars like prisoners. Leaning against the fence, she gazed at the animals and blinked back a tear. She was so caught up with the plight of these wild horses she didn't hear him come up behind her.

"What are you doing here?" Josh Gentry asked.

Her mouth fell open in surprise, and she banged her chin against the top metal bar of the fence. She bit back a cry of surprise. He already considered her a first-class klutz. No need to add fuel to the fire. She turned to face him.

"Same thing I was doing at your ranch. Looking for the Wild Mustang Man."

He surveyed her with an unmistakably disapproving gaze. "Don't you ever give up?"

"Give up? I just got here."

"So I noticed."

He noticed. Now was the time to strike. "I was wondering…"

"You look a little better," he said, tilting her chin forward with his thumb and forefinger to get a better look at her eye.

His touch sent shivers up her spine even in the hot Nevada sunshine His face was so close she could see glints of green in his blue eyes. "Thank you." She was proud of how even her voice was, while her heart beat double time. "Have you…have you had a chance to think over my proposal?"

He was silent so long that hope began to surge in her heart. The whinnying of the horses and clouds of dust filled the air, but she scarcely noticed. He'd changed his mind. He must have. Why else would he stand there studying her with his eyebrows knotted together. "Swelling's gone down, bruise fading, yes, a definite improvement."

"That's nice of you to say, but—"

"I didn't say it to be nice," he said.

"I know, but…" She was getting desperate. How long was he going to stand there and stare at her and talk about her looks? What did he see when he looked at her besides the bruises and the swelling? Just a city girl come to interfere with his way of life? What she saw was a virile, sexy horseman who she needed in the worst way to make a go of her fledgling company.

"About my proposal," she continued.

"The answer is no. Absolutely not. You can go home now."

"I'm not going home until I find my Wild Mustang Man." She gave a cursory glance around at the ranchers huddled in groups around the corral, who were pointing at this horse and that, loudly discussing their merits. But none of them looked like her Wild Mustang Man. None of them looked like Josh Gentry.

"Want me to introduce you to any of the guys?" he asked, noting her interest with a mocking smile.

She straightened her shoulders. "No, thanks. I can manage on my own." With that she strode off purposefully toward a knot of wranglers, reminding herself that the future of her business rested on finding the right man for the product. At this point all she wanted to do was escape the scrutiny of Mr. Gentry and show him she didn't need him. To do that she would have walked into a den of lions. Instead she walked into a den of cowboys.

"Um...excuse me, gentlemen?"

They suddenly stopped talking and stared at her.

"I was wondering—" Oh, Lord, she couldn't, she just couldn't talk about men's cologne to this group. She could tell by the looks on their faces it was completely out of the question. They would laugh her right out of there. "I was wondering if you could advise me on a horse to buy."

"Why, shore," one man said, tipping his hat politely. "What didja have in mind?"

"In mind? Why, something gentle, I mean—"

Their raucous laughter drowned out her words.

"Honey, you come to the wrong place for a gentle horse. See, these here horses are wild. You gotta go to one hell of a lot of work to tame them, and even then they might not be what you'd call gentle."

"I see," Bridget said, nodding thoughtfully. "Well, thank you. I appreciate your advice. It was nice, um...talking to you." With a polite smile she backed away and walked quickly to the other side of the corral, trying to lose herself in the crowd, hoping, praying that Josh had left and had not witnessed the fiasco she had just initiated.

Josh was supposed to be looking for a horse. That was why he was there, after all, but his attention was not on the horseflesh in the corral. He couldn't tear his eyes from the woman in the slim new jeans and the form-fitting T-shirt who was making her way around the corral. He wasn't the only one watching her. Other men watched—they not only watched, they stopped her, smiled at her and spoke to her.

He shouldn't be surprised. She was the best-looking woman to arrive on the scene in Harmony, Nevada, for some time. Maybe ever. She stood out like a long-stemmed red rose in the midst of a hayfield.

Had she found her stupid Wild Mustang Man yet? He hoped so. He hoped she'd convinced some poor fool to do it so she'd leave him alone and he could get back to whatever it was he did in his real life.

She was talking to Tex Woodruff at that very moment. He'd taken his hat off and he was looking at her as if she was just the prettiest little thing he'd ever seen. That's probably what he was saying to her, if he knew Tex. The man had a mustache a mile wide and a line a mile long. Not a bad rider though. He'd make a great Wild Mustang Man. Which had probably occurred to her by now. Which was why she was still talking to him after five minutes. She was looking up at him as if he'd assured her he was the greatest rider in the West. He *was* good. Josh didn't like the way he treated his horses, though. Didn't much like the way he treated his women, either, if rumor was correct.

She was reaching into her pocket, pulling out one of her business cards, the same kind she'd given him. Giving the same pitch she'd given him. Tex was smiling, nodding, spending about ten minutes studying her card. Guy probably couldn't read. Who cared? Who said the Wild Mustang Man had to read? As Josh understood it, it wasn't a speaking part. But it was *his* part. She'd offered it to him first. And by God, no simple-minded wrangler was going to take it away from him.

Without thinking any further, Josh plowed through the crowd, towering over most of the other men he passed as he made his way to where Bridget was talking to Tex. With a brief nod to Tex, he took Bridget by the elbow and spun her around.

"Still looking for your Wild Mustang Man?"

Her eyes widened. "Yes, but—"

"Then I'll do it. Let's go." With his hand firmly on her elbow they walked through the crowd, leaving a bewildered Tex standing there staring, as they marched past the milling horseflesh out into the parking lot to Josh's truck and horse trailer where he finally stopped. Bridget turned to face him, out of breath, with her eyes shining.

"Did you say you'd do it? You'd be my Wild Mustang Man?"

"You're sure it won't take up my time?" he asked gruffly, already regretting his decision.

"Absolutely not. We'll shoot around your schedule."

"We?"

"The camera crew. They'll just be here at the very end. You're the boss, though. Whatever you say goes. What...what made you change your mind?"

He tried to think of an answer. The hot sun beating mercilessly on his head was no help. Sweat trickled down his forehead. He opened his truck and reached into his cooler for two bottles of ginger beer. He'd never admit to anyone, not even to himself, that he was jealous of some half-baked cowboy. He handed her a cold drink, opened his and took a long swallow.

"The part about Max's college education," he said at last. "I wish now I'd gone on to college. But there was the ranch. And there was Molly."

"Molly's your wife?"

"Was my wife until she died two years ago."

"I'm sorry," Bridget said softly.

"Have you ever been married?" he asked to change the subject.

"No. I came close once. I was engaged last year, but I'm not anymore. I'm on my own. My own business, my own life. I like it that way," she said in a determined tone, then tilted her chin and took a long drink of ginger beer.

Fascinated he watched a drop trickle from the corner of her mouth. Almost reached over to catch it. Stopped himself just in time. But couldn't stop his heartbeat from accelerating.

"Well, anyway," he said, slamming the door to his truck. "I came here to get a horse. I better get back in there before they're picked over." Or before he'd spilled his guts to an advertising lady from the city who exuded self-sufficiency and the essence of exotic flowers that teased his nostrils, making him think of silk sheets and satin skin. Hers. What was wrong with him? He was a cotton sheet and calluses kind of guy. And she was *not* his type.

"Wait a minute," Bridget said, realizing she was being dismissed before she was ready to go. Yes, she got what she came for, but she wasn't ready to leave. Not yet. "If it's not asking too much, I'd like to see how you choose a wild mustang. For research purposes, you know. I haven't shot many pictures yet, either. So if it's all right with you…" She could tell by his expression it wasn't all right, but he resignedly tossed his empty bottle and hers into the truck, and they went back inside to where the wild horses were waiting to be chosen.

Leaning next to him at the fence, her shoulder brushed his. Even through his chambray shirt, she could feel the hard muscle there. The herd of horses behind the fence blurred, and all she could do was imagine how her Wild Mustang Man would look without the shirt, all sun-bronzed muscle and flat, washboard stomach…. Her pulse rate shot up, and her cheeks reddened. She slid a glance in his direction. He was looking at the horses, watching them snort and jerk their heads. Didn't give her a glance.

So this strange attraction she felt was completely one-sided. It was just as well. If they were going to work together, she couldn't afford to get involved with him. Combining work and romance didn't work. Led to disastrous results. If the truth were known, she'd choose romance any day. But she had no choice any longer. Her ex-fiancé, Scott, had found her lacking as a desirable woman and as an account executive. Okay, so he didn't want to marry her. But he was wrong in saying she was no good at advertising. She was.

She'd show him. She'd show everyone, because after landing the dream account, she'd just signed the dream man to be its symbol. She couldn't lose—as long as she kept her wits about her. Deliberately she broke the contact and moved several inches to her left.

"I don't understand how you can stand to do this," she said, keeping her eyes on the horses. "These are wild creatures, right? Used to running free in the Nevada desert. Now they're trapped behind bars. Like prisoners. They'll never roam free again."

"They'll also never be attacked by mountain lions again or starve from lack of feed. They'll get good care, get rid of their parasites and live longer in captivity."

She let his words sink in and felt better about the plight of the horses. "I didn't know that."

"Most people outside this area don't know it. They feel sorry for the horses, just like you do. They think we resell them for dog food."

"That's awful. What the Wild Mustang Association needs is better publicity. So the world will know what you're doing here," she said. It would be a labor of love for someone. Someone who loved horses, who loved their spirit, who appreciated them for what they were, a throwback to simpler, frontier times. "What do these people want them for?" she asked with a glance at the prospective buyers.

"Pleasure, riding, packing. You can be sure if they're willing to take on a horse who's never even been haltered before, they're going to look after them."

"Then all that talk about selling them to glue factories..." she said.

"It happened. But that was before the Wild Horse Act."

"Of 1971."

He shot her a surprised glance. "You've done your homework."

She smiled. It wasn't really a compliment, but it might be as close as he came. It gave her an unreasonably warm feeling around her heart. Which was spoiled by his next remark.

"How do you like the smell?"

She wrinkled her nose. It was the smell of 150 horses penned together—the sweat, the manure, the dirt, all combined.

"Is that what Wild Mustang cologne smells like?" he asked, nudging her with his elbow.

She straightened. "Of course not. It's not quite as...as earthy. But it has all the elements. The pungency... the...you know," she finished weakly. She couldn't deny that the smell of the wild mustangs was something no man would want to deliberately apply to his body and no woman would want her man to smell like. But who among the millions of women at the men's cologne counters would know that? "It's the image that counts."

"And not the reality?" he asked.

She didn't answer. She wasn't going to get into a discussion on the value of advertising. She had a feeling she could never convince him of the validity of her field. But he'd agreed to be a part of her ad campaign, for whatever reason, and that was enough of a victory for one day. She waited a few minutes, letting his question hang in the air, before she asked one of her own.

"How can you tell...how do you decide which horse to choose?"

"I look to see if they have a bright eye."

Bridget studied the fast-moving horses that milled in front of them and shook her head, unable to differentiate one from the other. "What's a bright eye?" she asked.

"It's when they're curious," he said, pointing to a black horse with a white star on its forehead. "Watch this one. This is one I'd buy. Look how curious he is about us. He's looking us over, reserving judgment, but he's not out and out scared like most of the others."

"I don't blame them," she said. "I'd be scared, too."

"You, scared?" he asked. "I can't imagine that. You put yourself in the path of a wild kid on a bike, you barge into his house and ask a stranger to be a Wild Mustang Man. What *does* scare you?" he asked.

She shrugged. Nobody had ever called her brave before. "I don't know. Snakes, spiders. Failure." This conversation was getting too close for comfort. She didn't want to talk about failure. She didn't want to talk about herself. She wanted to talk about horses. It was much safer. "Imagine being penned up after a lifetime of freedom," she said. She felt his curious gaze on her, but she stared straight ahead at the black horse in the corral.

"Does freedom mean so much to you?" he asked.

"I guess it does. I guess that's why I started my own ad agency. To have the freedom to do what I want."

"Is this what you want to do?" he asked.

"Of course it is. I'm having the time of my life."

"What about marriage, kids?"

Bridget swallowed hard. Just when she'd come across so convincing. He could have gone all day without asking that one. The questions were making her nervous, the last one especially. As nervous as those horses there, wondering what was going to become of them.

"No time for marriage and kids," she said lightly. "They're just not compatible with my job. When I work, I work around the clock. It's a competitive business. Always somebody else trying to take away your business when you're not looking. Besides, nobody gets everything they want,'' she said as an afterthought. As if he needed her to tell him that.

Up until recently she'd thought she might get everything—an interesting job followed by or in tandem with a husband she loved, a home and kids. Now that she knew it wasn't going to work out that way, she was free to pursue her career with all her energies. Which was not a bad thing. No, not at all.

"No...they don't,'' he muttered under his breath, then he turned his back to the horses. "I'm going to the office now and fill out the paperwork on the horse I want and pay the fees. I assume you have a ride back to town.''

So that was it. The end of this question-and-answer session. He'd cut her off before she had a chance to ask him anything. Like what was *he* afraid of, how much did freedom mean to *him* and what it was *he* really wanted to do. He'd taken steps in the opposite direction before she realized what was happening. He was leaving.

"Wait,'' she called, elbowing her way through the crowd. "When will you be home? Can I come by and take some pictures?''

He shrugged without turning around or even breaking stride, and she finally gave up, stopped in her tracks and turned toward the parking lot, realizing that she'd gotten all she was going to get out of him for now. And that he'd somehow found out more about her than most people knew, her friends included.

Chapter Three

Josh drove home slowly, with one eye on his horse trailer and his newest wild mustang. He was pleased about the horse. She was the right age, between two and three years old, and had good potential. Two of the first four horses he'd bought some ten years ago were still working. The other two were retired in the pasture, and they'd earned it. Countless others had been trained and sold and had provided him with a decent living.

He could ride, he could break horses, he could train them. But what he was best at, what he was proudest of, was his ability to choose them. To pick out a horse in that milling, constantly moving herd took a good eye, sound judgment and a knowledge of horseflesh. He hadn't made many mistakes, and he was proud of that.

He wasn't so proud of his major life decisions. Skipping college. Getting married and settling down at eighteen. Allowing Max the freedom to run wild on the ranch. And now this. Agreeing to become a symbol for a men's cologne. What would the people in Harmony say when they found out? Hopefully the ad campaign would be a big flop, so they wouldn't find out. If they did, he'd tell them it was only to benefit Max's college education.

At this rate, however, the boy would be lucky to graduate from Harmony High School. Tearing up the front lawn doing wheelies. Running over innocent women. A vision of Bridget in her linen shorts and her black eye, uncomplaining as he pressed an ice pack on her eyelid, made his heart thud in his chest. He would never admit it to anybody, but he'd had an uncontrollable desire at that moment to take her in his arms and tell her she was going to be all right. Fortunately he was able to control that uncontrollable desire, or God knows where he'd be. Probably in court for sexual harassment.

For one crazy moment as he'd watched her lower lip tremble when he dismissed her from his house, he had wanted nothing more than to haul her back into the house and kiss her. He'd repressed the feeling until now. Denied that it ever happened. It was useless to think about it, to relive it. The only rational explanation was that it had been so long, so damned long since he'd kissed a woman. Since he'd seen a woman blush. Since he'd desired a woman.

Not that he desired Bridget McCloud. She was not his type.

He reached into his shirt pocket and pulled out her wrinkled card. What was that doing there? He remembered distinctly stuffing it in his pants pocket. And that was days ago. He pressed it to his nose and inhaled her scent which still clung tenaciously. Like Bridget herself. Clinging tenaciously to the idea that he was going to be her Wild Mustang Man. The card only reminded him that she didn't know the meaning of the word *no*. That there was no stopping her once she had an idea in her head.

Though today he thought he'd gotten through to her, when he'd said that nobody would really want to smell like a wild mustang. He sure wouldn't. And he didn't think she would, either.

He grinned, remembering how she'd sputtered when he'd mentioned the smell of the horses. How her cheeks reddened, her spine stiffened. Teasing her, putting her on the spot, watching her reactions, was more fun than he'd had in years. The funny thing was the more she talked about herself the more he wanted to know. That was not part of the plan. *She* was not part of the plan.

Since Molly died, his plan was to get by. To make a living for himself and Max. To put a rein on the boy's energies and try to channel them into constructive paths. To keep Molly on a pedestal. To remember her as the perfect wife. His one and only wife. He hadn't looked at another woman since Molly died. Why bother? He'd pledged himself to her some fifteen years ago, and he would never go back on his honor. As he told his father, she would have done the same for him.

So why was he grinning like a jackal as he drove down the highway toward home, thinking about some city girl who was more interested in image than substance? Who was more at home at a perfume counter than at a 4-H meeting. Who put her career ahead of getting married and having a family. He didn't understand that. If Max's devotion to her was an indication, she'd make a good mother.

He shook his head. What business was it of his if she became the mother to a set of quintuplets? They were going to have a working relationship, the looser the better. She'd assured him he could continue his work, to lead his life. She'd better be right. Because he had no intention of turning his life around to promote a perfume...cologne...whatever.

When he got home, her car was in the driveway and she was sitting on his front steps. He swore under his breath, made a sharp turn without acknowledging her presence and headed for the barn, the horse trailer bouncing behind him. When he got out of his truck, she was there, camera in hand. Was there no escaping this woman?

"I hope you don't mind," she said, snapping pictures of him and the horse while he backed it up, kicking and snorting, out of the trailer.

"I do mind," he said throwing a halter over the horse's head. "This is a very sensitive time for the horse. If you get kicked, I won't be responsible."

"I understand that," she said, backing up only very slightly. "But this is all so interesting and so important for the whole mustang story."

He didn't answer. He tried to ignore her, but she was everywhere, in the barn, outside the barn, in the chute, with her camera clicking away. Until he heard his mother's car pull up in front of the house. And Max's voice in the distance. Then and only then did she walk around the barn and disappear from view. Josh could only imagine how happy Max would be to see Bridget, while *he* couldn't be happier to see her leave. He only hoped she would have gone back to town by the time he finished up in the barn.

A short time later his mother found him sitting on top of his fence chewing on a stalk of grass watching his new horse race around the corral.

"There you are," she said. "I left you a shepherd's pie for your dinner, a salad and a rhubarb crisp."

"Sounds good."

"There's plenty if your friend wants to stay."

He glanced at his mother. Her expression was bland, no hidden meaning, no hidden agenda. At least he hoped not.

"She's not my friend," he explained.

"Max's friend, then," she said.

"Don't tell me," he said shaking his head in despair. "He's already asked her to dinner."

His mother smiled. "I thought I ought to warn you."

"Sounds like it's too late."

"Is there something wrong with her?" his mother asked.

"Oh, no, there's nothing wrong with her. Nothing at all. She's going to be here for God knows how long, nosing around, interfering with my work, taking pictures of me and the wild mustangs for some damned perfume commercial."

"Really? How exciting."

"You think so? How would you like somebody dogging you night and day, making a pest of herself, getting in your way?"

"I don't know," his mother said. "It might be good for you to have some adult company."

"*Some* adult company? There's going to be a whole camera crew here eventually. And why do I need company, by the way? Am I turning into some kind of hermit?" he asked.

"Of course not. It's just that your father and I—"

"I know, he already told me. You want me to get on with my life. Find somebody to replace Molly. I'm not going to do that. I was in love once. I'm not ever going to fall in love again. Especially with someone who doesn't belong here."

"I'm not talking about your falling in love again," she explained gently. "I'm talking about inviting someone to dinner."

"Fine. Invite her to dinner. Invite the whole ad agency to dinner if you want."

"It's not what I want. It's what Max wants. I only want what's best for you. I can't help thinking you ought to expand your circle of acquaintances to include a few more people than horses."

"Okay, okay, she can stay to dinner. Are you happy now?" he asked his mother.

"Delirious," she acknowledged, favoring him with a

fond smile. "Let me know how it turns out. The shepherd's pie, I mean."

That's not what she meant at all, he thought, watching her go. His mother was an incurable romantic and wouldn't rest until Josh had found someone else, a mother for Max, a mate for himself. She'd left him alone until this year, then she'd started dropping hints about various women in town who were single or divorced. Up to now he'd ignored her successfully. But tonight she had a look in her eye he hadn't seen before. A look of quiet determination.

When he finally got his horse settled down, he reluctantly made his way to the house where he bumped into Ms. Ad Agency Exec of the Year.

"Oh, I was just leaving," she said, her hand on the doorknob.

"I thought you were staying for dinner."

"You did?" There was no mistaking the way her eyes lit up; she was pleasantly surprised he hadn't shoved her out the door. Maybe he did need more adult company. "No," she said, "I couldn't intrude."

He wiped the dirt off his forehead with his handkerchief. "What's the matter, don't you like shepherd's pie?"

"I love shepherd's pie. I mean I think I'd love it. I've never had it. It looks wonderful."

"You're here. You might as well stay."

"If you're sure...."

"I'm going to wash up," he said and walked down the hall to the bathroom.

Bridget sat on the edge of the plain pine kitchen chair. Was it possible that she'd been invited to dinner at the very house she'd been summarily dismissed from only a few days ago? Of course *he* hadn't invited her. His son had. But he hadn't objected. At this point she was grateful for small favors.

The conversation at the dinner table was minimal. But

the food was great. His mother was a wonderful cook. She told him so.

"It sure beats the food at the diner in town," she said enthusiastically accepting a second helping.

He gave her a sharp look as he served himself another large helping, and she realized what she'd said could be misconstrued as a hint she'd prefer to eat there with him.

"Of course it's a wonderful way to learn about the town. People are so friendly and talkative," she added. He didn't say anything. Maybe he thought she was comparing him unfavorably with the gregarious crowd at the café. "That's where I heard about the wild horse sale. At breakfast this morning."

"Uh-huh."

Breakfast, such a long time ago. In the interim she'd signed up the perfect Wild Mustang Man, learned about wild mustangs, but not much about the man. Which was okay. It wasn't necessary to get into his background. She'd met his son and his mother. She'd seen the inside of his bathroom and was now eating dinner across the table from him. What more did she want?

"Can I be excused?" Max asked, hopping down from his chair.

His father looked surprised at his sudden display of manners. "Yeah, sure. I guess so."

"I gotta try out my new slingshot. I promised Bridget I'd show her how to use it. Then I gotta show her how to ride a bike."

She smiled as he ran out the back door. "I feel like I've missed a lot growing up in the city."

"Never had a slingshot?" he asked, raising his eyebrows.

"Or a bike or a horse."

"What did you do for fun?"

"Um...I don't know exactly. I'm sure I never had as much fun as Max."

"Or get injured as often as Max," he said.

"Oh, no, I never got injured. My mother wouldn't have permitted it. Mothers can be terribly overprotective. Mine was."

"I worry about Max. Maybe I'm not protective enough."

"Seems to me he's turning out fine. He's a lot of fun." She stood and looked out the kitchen window to watch him race across the grass, falling head over heels and picking himself up in pursuit of a pebble he'd lanced from his slingshot. "I envy you," she said softly. He didn't say anything, though he must have wondered what she meant. Hadn't she told him today that she wasn't interested in marriage and children, that they were incompatible with a career in advertising? She'd told herself that so often she almost believed it. The room was quiet, so quiet she could hear the ticking of the grandfather clock in the living room. Long shadows fell over the fields that stretched as far as the eye could see. His land. His son. His life. Why did that make her feel melancholy? As if he had everything and she had nothing? She had a great job and great friends back in San Francisco, and to top it off she'd had a wonderful day.

"Thanks for the dinner," she said over her shoulder. "I'll go out for a brief slingshot lesson, then I've really got to go."

She pushed the back door open.

"By the way," he said. "I hope you got enough pictures, because I'm going to be busy tomorrow." There was no mistaking the firm determination in his voice. He didn't want to see her tomorrow. She didn't dare ask about the next day.

"Me, too," she said, and stepped outside into the warm summer evening. "I'm going to be busy, too." He wasn't the only one who'd be busy. She had no idea what she'd be doing, but by heaven, she knew she'd be busy. Horses whinnied in the distance. Max shouted to her and beckoned eagerly when he saw her, which warmed her heart. It was nice to know there was one Gentry who wanted her there.

While Bridget watched, Max put a half dozen empty soda cans on a log. Then he took Bridget's hand and marched her to a patch of lawn he'd marked off with string. He stood next to her, shot a pebble at the cans and missed by an inch. "Dad gum it," he grumbled.

"That was close," she said.

"I been practicing all afternoon. I still haven't hit a can. Now it's your turn," he said handing her his slingshot.

"But, Max," she protested, turning the slingshot over in her hand. "I can't do this. I haven't the slightest idea—" A leather strip, two pieces of rubber and a smooth wooden handle. She hadn't a clue what to do with it.

"Here's a pebble," he said. "You put it there in the leather, pull back and let her rip."

Bridget did what he said. The pebble fell to the ground at her feet.

Max shook his head and handed her another. The same thing happened. Bridget sighed, wishing she could make a graceful exit. But Max was looking up at her so hopefully, she had to try again. She didn't glance at the house. She didn't want to know if Josh was watching her. Somehow she knew he was. She felt his eyes on her. His curious gaze. He didn't understand her. Sometimes she didn't understand herself. She was a bundle of contradictions. A hard-driving businesswoman who was getting used to the silence of the country, to the wide open spaces.

Of course she didn't understand him, either. A man who was more accustomed to horses than humans. A man who changed his mind about being her Wild Mustang Man in the blink of an eyelash.

Not that it mattered if he watched her like a hawk watching its prey. If he had nothing better to do than to stare out the window watching her fail at some childish sport, that was his problem. As for her, she was going to stand there until she succeeded. If it took all night. But having someone gaze at her from afar made it twice as hard. Her hands shook as she yanked on the rubber band once again. And once again saw the pebble fall to the ground.

"You know what? I'm not getting the hang of this," she confessed to Max. "Maybe I ought to try again some other—"

"What's the problem?" Suddenly Josh was stalking across the lawn toward them.

"Nothing, I—"

"You show her, Dad," Max said.

Josh stepped behind her and put his arms around her. His chest was rock solid. His heart beat loud and steady, right through his shirt. The muscles in his arms held her strong and steady. She held her breath. What was she supposed to do now? It was hard enough concentrating on hitting a target without him holding her like that and making her heart race. Fortunately she didn't have to concentrate. All she had to do was follow orders.

"Now, hold on tight. Like this." He wrapped his hands around hers, molding her left hand around the handle, the right around the leather strip.

She prayed he wouldn't notice how damp her palms were and how her fingers trembled. Or if he did, that he'd chalk it up to learning a new skill. That's all it was. Just nerves. Just wanting to succeed. Just wanting to lean back against him, feel his arms tighten around her, close her eyes and forget all about the slingshot. But she couldn't. They were waiting, both of them. Waiting to see her do it.

"Pebble," Josh said.

Max handed him a pebble.

"Insert pebble," he ordered, his warm breath ruffling her hair.

"How am I supposed to do that?" she asked. "I'd need a third hand."

"Here," he said and inserted the pebble in the leather strip for her. "Now aim. Get the target centered between the two prongs of the slingshot. Got it?"

"Yes," she said. At that point she would have agreed to anything.

"Shoot."

She shot. The pebble hit the can. She exhaled softly. "Beginner's luck," she said.

Max laughed with joy and jumped into the air. Then he ran to gather new pebbles.

"Was that so hard?" Josh asked. His lips brushed her ear. The pebble had been lanced, had hit its target, but his arms were still wrapped around her.

"Nothing to it," she said under her breath, wishing she could stay there forever, or at least a few more minutes. She'd never felt so safe, so secure and yet so scared in her life. Scared that she might get to like this—being held, being a part of a family; shooting at targets in the evening as dusk fell over the fields and the sun set behind the hill, the same hill where she'd first seen him outlined against the clear blue Nevada sky; then going back into the house for coffee as the lights went on inside and night settled around the house.

But she wasn't going back in the house. Not for coffee, not for anything. She hadn't been invited. She didn't belong there. They were a family, and she was not part of it. She didn't want to be. She was happy being on her own. Lucky for her, because she had terrible judgment when it came to men. Witness her close encounter with Scott. Kate told her he was no good. Others told her the same thing. Here in Nevada she was on her own. Nobody to tell her who was

Mr. Right For Her and who wasn't. She had to rely on her own judgment. Which was faulty.

She knew she should break out of his arms and leave, but she didn't. Not when she fit there so well. Aware of every muscle and bone in his body. Aware of every breath he took. Aware of his chin resting on top of her head. Watching the sun set in the west. Wanting it to go on forever. But it didn't. Max came running up with a handful of pebbles and she gave a guilty start.

The boy shot them both a curious look. "You can let go of her now, Dad. She hit the target. Didja see it?"

"I saw it," he said, dropping his arms slowly so that his hands brushed her supersensitive skin.

She stumbled forward, as if she'd just been released from a hospital bed. She took a few steps toward the driveway. Toward her car and toward safety.

"I think I'll quit while I'm ahead," she explained to both of them with a weak smile. Max looked disappointed, Josh looked relieved, and she had no idea how *she* looked. She knew how she felt, though. Shaky, confused and embarrassed. First she'd stayed for dinner, to Josh's dismay, then she'd got lost in his embrace, which wasn't an embrace at all.

Bridget drove back to town with her camera case full of exposed film to develop. If her pictures turned out half as well as she hoped, the Wild Mustang people would be ecstatic and start throwing money at the project. She and Kate could put furniture in their office, order stationery, light fixtures. And all thanks to Josh Gentry.

The next day she packaged her film and express mailed it to Kate with instructions to let her know the instant it was developed. Then she went to the laundromat. After she put her clothes in the washing machine she sat down to watch the people walk down Main Street. So that's what it was like to live in Harmony, Nevada, she thought. Yesterday she thought it was colorful and picturesque. Today it was tedious and boring. Could it have anything to do with Josh Gentry? Yesterday she'd been with him, today she was alone.

She'd better get used to being alone, because he didn't want her hanging around every day, and she didn't know anyone else in town. She watched enviously as two women about her age passed the laundromat window, laughing and talking. One was tall, very pretty with long, dark hair. The other was a cute little blond, the kind who was probably a cheerleader in high school. They glanced in at Bridget as they passed, and she smiled wistfully, wishing she knew someone to talk to, to share gossip, to confide in. She desperately needed a friend. Someone to tell her she wasn't crazy to have a crush on a man she scarcely knew.

In a minute the two women came back by the window, stopped for a moment, then entered.

"Excuse me," the little blond said, "are you...you're not the woman from the ad agency who's going to turn Josh Gentry into a sex symbol, are you?"

"I am from an ad agency, but I don't know about turning him into a...a..." What was wrong with her, why couldn't she say the word?

"Don't listen to her," the tall, pretty woman said. "The word is he's going to be the star of a commercial you're making."

"That's true. At least that's the plan." Bridget was so desperate for some companionship, she stuck out her hand and introduced herself, something she never would have done with strangers in a laundromat in San Francisco. She learned the tall woman was Tally and her friend was Suzy.

"Why don't we go somewhere and talk?" Suzy said. "How about coffee at the diner?"

Bridget threw her clothes into a dryer and joined the other women for a short walk down Main Street.

"So tell us all about life in San Francisco," Suzy said.

"How did you know...?"

"Word travels fast in a small town. My mother saw Josh's mother at church, and that's how I heard."

"I see. Well, it's not very different from life here," Bridget said. "I go to work. I go to the laundromat. Have coffee with friends." Tally held the door open for her and the three of them took a booth in the corner.

"I'll bet you don't live in a rented room on Main Street. I'll bet you have one of those old Victorians, what do they call them, painted ladies?" Tally said.

"I wish I did. I live in an ordinary apartment. It does have a nice view of the bridge and the bay, but other than that it's nothing special. Tell me about yourselves. Are you natives?" Bridget asked.

"Harmony born and bred, both of us," Tally said. "Lived here all our lives. Graduated from Harmony High School with Josh."

"And Molly," Suzy added.

"What was she like?" Bridget asked quickly before she lost her nerve. It was none of her business, but she'd been curious about Josh's wife since she saw her picture on the mantel in the living room of the ranch house. This might be her only chance to find out about her. She certainly couldn't ask Josh. "Were you good friends?"

"We were friends," Tally said. "But not good friends. Molly didn't have any close girlfriends. She didn't need any. She had Josh. And she was...how shall I say this—"

"She was perfect," Suzy said. "She sewed all her own clothes, Max's too, knit sweaters for Josh, grew all their vegetables and put up enough for winter. Whenever there was an emergency, she was there. You could count on her to help deliver a baby or a calf. That's the kind of person she was. Wasn't she, Tally?"

"Too good to be true," Tally murmured. "I must admit I was jealous of her sometimes. Especially that night after the senior prom when we all went to the beach. It seemed to me she had everything I wanted—a family, a ranch, horses, and a boyfriend who was crazy about her. She and Josh were the perfect couple. She was the prom princess. He was captain of the football team and class president. I was nothing. Not that *she* made me feel that way," she assured Bridget. "She was kind and thoughtful, too. Assured me the wish I made on a star would come true. She was right."

"Well, mine hasn't come true yet," Suzy said with a mock pout. "See, Molly made us all wish on a falling star that night. I wished for a husband and a baby, Tally wanted a Thoroughbred horse, and Molly, she only wanted to be married to Josh."

"And to win first place for her jam at the county fair," Tally reminded her. "Which she did."

"All her dreams came true. And then she died," Suzy said, and picked up her coffee cup. There was a respectful silence around the table.

"Sometimes I think Josh died, too," Tally said. "He certainly withdrew into a shell. He didn't come to our fifteenth reunion. We never see him anymore."

"You would have buried yourself, too," Suzy said, "if it had been Jed who'd died."

Tally sipped her coffee thoughtfully. "I wonder. I think eventually I would have come out of it. I think you would have forced me to come out of it," she said to Suzy.

"That's what friends are for," Suzy said. "Hey, Tally. Maybe it's our fault Josh has become a recluse. You know how men are. They rely on women to set up the social situations. We haven't forced him back out into the world. We've let him drift away. Hmm." Then she turned to Bridget. "Anyway tell us how you talked Josh into posing for an ad, when he's been a hermit these past years? You must have done something. He's not susceptible to flattery or flirting. God knows, every single woman in town has tried, except me, of course. I know better.''

"It wasn't easy," Bridget admitted, her head still reeling from the image of Molly, the perfect homemaker and Josh's perfect wife. No wonder he was still single and likely to remain so—Molly was a hard act to follow. Darned near impossible. Not that she'd try. Not on a bet. "Being the spokesman for a particular product like Wild Mustang men's cologne—''

"That's the name of the cologne?" Suzy asked.

Bridget nodded, waiting for the kind of derisive comment Josh had made about the smell of wild mustangs.

But Suzy's blue eyes sparkled. "That sounds so sexy. I can see it now. Josh, bare chested, riding a wild mustang bareback in the commercials.''

Bridget nodded eagerly, grateful for the positive reinforcement, but she also felt a pang of jealousy. "Are you sure you're not interested in him?" she asked Suzy.

Suzy shook her head. "Not me. I know better than to compete with a saint, especially one who's in heaven, still sewing, knitting, canning and helping out at harvest time. Besides, Josh is like a brother to me. At least he was until he pulled this disappearing act. Go ahead, you were saying...''

"Oh, yes," Bridget continued. "Being a spokesman for a product can be very rewarding financially. I mentioned he could make enough for Max's college education.''

"That Max is a handful," Tally said. "Have you met him?''

"I ran into him the first day I got here, or rather he ran into me, on his bicycle. He's a cute kid.''

"No kids of your own?" Suzy asked.

"No kids, no husband," Bridget said. "Advertising is a

tough, competitive field. It takes a lot of time and effort to make it. I just started out on my own this year. No time for marriage now. Maybe someday when I'm ready to retire and take it easy. I just read about two eighty-year-olds who met in a nursing home and fell in love. That'll be me," she said lightly, as if she didn't care about getting married anytime soon. Which was the truth. It would probably take her about fifty years to get over her fears of letting herself love anyone again. Which would take her right up into her eighties.

"Maybe that's what I should do," Suzy said. "Of course it will be too late for me to have kids." She sighed loudly.

"Anybody who's as bright and cute as you are will find somebody anyday now," Tally said. "You too, Bridget. Don't tell me there aren't men beating down your door in San Francisco?"

"Not exactly," Bridget said. "And I must admit after attending the wild horse sale the other day and getting a look at the men around here, it makes city men look awfully effete, if you know what I mean."

Tally and Suzy exchanged a brief, meaningful look. Bridget hoped she hadn't given anything away. With gossip spreading like wildfire in this town she didn't want anyone saying or even thinking she was even moderately interested in Josh or anyone else. Which she wasn't. She was just curious. About him, about his former wife and any other detail that contributed to her understanding of her Wild Mustang Man. Not hers, she reminded herself. If all went well, soon he'd belong to the world.

"Anyway," Suzy continued, "even with the money, I'm surprised he agreed to do it. So is everybody in town."

"So am I," Bridget confessed. "But I promised to make it as painless as possible. Just taking pictures of him at work. No posing. Nothing artificial."

"I can't wait to see the pictures," Tally said.

"And smell the cologne," Suzy added. "I've got to get back to work now, ladies. It was good meeting you, Bridget. Let's do this again. If you have time, that is."

"I will. I won't be able to spend all day photographing," Bridget said. As much as she'd like to, Josh would never permit it.

From the diner they each went their separate ways. Bridget went back to the laundromat to stare thoughtfully at the clothes flopping around in the dryer, to think about Josh Gentry, his son and his former wife. The hours dragged, but somehow she got through the day, and the next day she called Kate to find out how the pictures had turned out.

"They're great, just great," Kate said. "I ran them by the client this morning and they loved them. They want some closeups, though, before they sign the contract. They say they need to see his face, from all angles. I need to see it, too. This guy is really something."

"Didn't I tell you?" Bridget asked. Then she sighed loudly. "His face from all angles. Okay, okay. I'll go out there right now." She crossed her fingers on both hands that he'd be home.

"We're close, Bridgie," Kate said. "We're getting close. I can feel it, can't you?"

"I think so," she said. But standing on the quiet street of this small town in a remote corner of Nevada, she felt far removed from the frantic world of advertising. Not that she wasn't eager to succeed. She was. She wanted to show Scott he was wrong about her, that she was good at what she did. She could write copy, take pictures and sell products. She could support herself. Which was fortunate because nobody else was going to support her.

It was a hard idea to get used to, but she would. She couldn't have the husband, house and family she'd always wanted. She'd have to be content with money, prestige, independence, and professional accolades. Provided *for* herself and *by* herself. There was only one person she could depend upon, and that was Bridget McCloud.

She uncrossed her fingers, hung up the phone and headed back to the ranch to face Josh Gentry once again and to shove a camera into his handsome face. Because if she didn't do it, who would?

Chapter Four

Josh had been busy yesterday. Very busy. There was no reason to feel guilty because he had things to do and didn't want to be interrupted. That woman was just going to have to realize he had work to do and couldn't spend all his time posing for pictures. Or teaching her how to shoot a slingshot. He kept thinking of the look on her face when he told her not to come by. A brief look of surprise, then a quick cover-up, a proud tilt of the chin, and low and behold she was busy, too. In the high desert dawn, he leaned against the narrow chute next to his corral and steadied his newest wild horse.

"Come on, babe. Don't be afraid. I'm not going to hurt you," he murmured waiting his chance to throw a halter on her. She was a proud little critter, with excellent possibilities. Just like Bridget.

Dammit, why couldn't he get that woman out of his mind? Why did everything remind him of her? He'd even dreamed about her the past two nights. One night was understandable. After all, she was the first woman who'd penetrated his home and his defenses since Molly died. But two nights in a row? And each dream more erotic than the last.

Then Max had to ask about her every day. Where was she, when was she coming back. He wanted to show her how good he was with his slingshot, how he could ride his bike no-handed down the driveway. He wanted her to see Barney, his pet rat. Fortunately Max had gone to play with a friend today, so he could finally get some peace and quiet and get to work. But he couldn't concentrate on haltering the horse.

Instead he was standing there staring off into space, thinking about Bridget. Remembering her sitting across the dinner table from him, not knowing what to say to her. Wanting her to go, yet wanting her to stay. Wondering when she was going to show up again with her camera around her neck, her tawny, windblown hair and her non-stop questions.

He looked around. Except for sound of hoof beats as his horses raced across the field in the distance, there was absolute silence. Just the way he liked it. But more than the silence, there was a hush in the air this morning. As if something was about to happen. Even his horse stopped stomping her hooves and pointed her ears forward, listening, waiting and watching. They were sensitive, the best of the wild mustangs, and this one was no exception. He smiled to himself. Yes, he'd made the right choice and got himself one hell of a good horse.

Why couldn't he be content with that? He'd been perfectly happy these past two years, raising Max and horses on his own. Well, maybe not happy, but content. Now, since *she'd* arrived, he wanted more. What exactly he wanted he refused to think about.

His mind drifted back to the other evening out on the grass when he'd seized an excuse to put his arms around her. He couldn't get over how soft and sweet she was. How she'd melted into his arms like warm taffy and stayed there. If it weren't for Max they might still be there, locked together, watching the sun set and rise and set again. Because he didn't want to let her go. He might be wrong but he didn't think she wanted to go, either. All the more reason not to encourage her. All the more reason to ignore her. Ignore a feisty package of guts and determination who at a moment's notice could turn deliciously sweet and supple in his arms? No way.

He glanced at the sky as if he could see Molly's puzzled face in the clouds. Talk about guilt. She'd never forgive him for such traitorous thoughts. "It won't happen again," he muttered to himself, and to Molly, too, if she was listening.

As if Molly was testing him, or maybe he was just testing himself, he heard the sound of a car in the distance. His horse heard it, too. It could have been anybody. But it wasn't. It was her. She pulled into his driveway and slammed her car door. He turned back to his horse, trying once again to halter her. But his horse was as jumpy as he was and refused his attempts.

When he glanced up she was there. Backlit against the sun, her body was outlined in gold sunlight. He shaded his eyes with his hand and stared at her as if she'd stepped out of his dream. But she was real, just as real as she'd been the other evening. Just as sexy and just as desirable and just as big a threat to his peace of mind.

He opened his mouth to say something like, "What do *you* want?"

But she spoke first.

"I'm sorry to bother you," she said.

"I'll bet," he muttered under his breath.

"But I need to take a few more pictures. If you don't mind."

"And if I do?"

"I still need them," she said. "You go ahead and do what you're doing. You won't even know I'm here."

Yeah, right, he thought, clenching his hands into fists.

"What *are* you doing?" she asked.

He shot her an irritated look.

"I'm sorry. I won't say another word."

"Sure."

"You think I talk a lot?" she asked, moving closer to take a picture.

"You promised not to bother me."

"How do I bother you?" she asked.

"You really want to know?"

"Yes, because…"

She never got to finish her sentence. He threw the halter on the ground and jerked her Zeiss Ikon from around her neck and set it on the fence post. She sucked in a sharp breath as his hands brushed against her breasts. Then with a ragged sound in the back of his throat, he hauled her into his arms and kissed her. She didn't resist. It was inevitable. She knew it as well as he did. This energy that flowed between them, that had been there since the first day she walked into his house, was too real to be ignored.

She kissed him back. He kissed her again and again. Each time deeper. Until their lips were fused and neither wanted to break apart. They clung to each other, wordlessly, mindlessly. Taking only a moment to come up for air, she parted her lips and welcomed him in. Their tongues met and tangled. He plunged deeper, looking for heaven knew what—fulfillment, warmth, acceptance….

He got all that and more. She was as warm and generous and passionate as in his dreams. She wound her arms around his neck, her hands tangling in his hair, pulling him down, bringing him closer still. Their bodies meshed as if they were made for each other. Her breasts were crushed against his chest, his arousal pressed against her belly. His heart thundered, drowning out the warning signals, drowning out the voice in his head that told him this was wrong. He wanted more. He wanted all of her. He was shocked at how badly he wanted her. So badly that in a far corner of his mind he considered taking her to the barn or to a haystack.

He slid his hands under her shirt to cup her breasts. So full, they fit so perfectly in his hands. She gasped and tugged at his shirt. Impatient, he lifted her off the ground. She wrapped her legs around his waist just like she'd done in his dreams. She caught her breath, then she kissed him again, this time light, feathery kisses along his jawline that made him so crazy with lust and longing that he actually started in the direction of the barn with her wrapped around his waist, her face buried in his neck.

If it hadn't been for his horse, whinnying and pawing the ground in a desperate attempt to get back into the corral, he didn't know what might have happened. Reluctantly he set Bridget on the top rail of the fence. She was breathing hard. His gaze dropped to her breasts where her nipples pressed against her shirt and gave away her body's response. He clenched his hands into fists to keep from lifting her right off that fence—the horse and the whole world be damned.

"I'm sorry," he said, his voice hoarse. "I was way out of line. I wasn't thinking. I got carried away. It's been so long...."

She gripped the railing so tightly her knuckles turned white. "It wasn't your fault."

"It won't happen again," he said.

"Because of..." Her voice trailed off.

"Because...that's the way it is. We get one chance at love, and I had mine. I was married to the most wonderful woman in the world. And then I lost her. It was the most painful experience anyone could ever go through. I would never... I could never take a chance on love again, never marry anyone again. Because you never know how fast things can change. How cruel life can be. I had everything, then in the blink of an eye, I had nothing. Except Max, of course. If it hadn't been for him, I couldn't have gone on living.''

"I see," Bridget said, looking away, but not before he saw her blink back a tear. Was that tear for him?

"Can you understand that?" he asked, his brow furrowed with concern.

"Of course, but it's been...how long?"

"It doesn't matter if it's been two years or twenty. I'll never forget the emptiness, the deep hole I couldn't climb out of." He shook his head, knowing he couldn't make her understand. No one could who hadn't gone through it.

"Is that what Molly would have wanted?" she asked, her eyes boring into his. "That you stay single and raise Max on your own?" she asked.

"I don't know. Probably not. It's not about Molly. It's about me and how I've pulled out of that black hole and how I never want to fall into it again. Do you know you sound like my father? But it's no good playing "what if." What if I'd died first? I'd want Molly to marry again. But the fact is she's dead and I'm here. I have to do what I have to do."

He clenched his hands into fists. Of course he would have wanted Molly to marry again, to find someone else. He wouldn't have wanted her to grow old alone. It was different for him. He liked being alone. He could almost see the years stretching ahead of him like a straight, four-lane highway. Imagined Max growing up, moving away and leaving him alone on the ranch. For some strange reason he felt an unexpected emptiness around his heart. What in the hell was wrong with him today? All this talk about the past and the tragedy that had left him alone had made him question his future, the future he thought held no surprises. Now he was starting to wonder.

"Would it make you feel any better to blame me for what just happened? We could go halves at least," she suggested with a wry smile.

He shook his head. In spite of his determination not to let Bridget tempt him, in spite of his apology, his treacherous gaze took another look at her, lingering on the swell of her breasts, remembering, despite his vow, how they'd felt in his hands. He imagined how she'd look without that shirt, without that lace bra. He would never know. "About the pictures," he said, yanking himself back to reality.

She hopped off the fence, took her camera and fiddled with the adjustments. Was it his imagination or were her hands shaking?

Bridget snapped a whole roll of film without knowing what she was doing. They might all be overexposed, like her feelings for Josh. They could be blurry and out of focus, which was how the world looked to her at this point. She didn't care. All she wanted to do was to get out of there before she made more of a fool of herself than she'd already done. She'd thrown herself at a man who was wedded to his mate forever. Like a humming bird—or was it a penguin? Destined to live out his life paying homage to her memory.

To fill the awkward silence while she took the pictures, she told Josh she'd met his old high school classmates.

"You didn't tell them about the men's cologne, did you?" he asked, his eyebrows drawn together in a frown.

"They already knew."

"Oh, fine. Now the whole town will know."

"It's a small town," she noted.

"You're observant."

"I'm sorry, but there are men who would be flattered to be chosen as the Wild Mustang Man."

"Well I'm not one of them."

"I understand that," she said stiffly. "But since you are the chosen one, at least I hope these pictures will convince the client that you are...."

Josh glanced off in the direction of his house. "Oh, Lord," he said. "It's my mother," he said. "Is that it? Are you finished?"

He doesn't want me to see her, or he doesn't want her to see me, she thought. "Yes, I'm finished. Don't worry. I won't tell anyone about this. And I promise to keep my hands off you from now on." She tried to give her words a light touch, but they came out sounding bitter. That's how she felt. She couldn't help it. She'd had a deeply moving experience, deeply sensual and erotic, she thought it might have meant something to him, but obviously it was just a release of tension. Or so he would have her believe.

"Keep your hands off," he muttered. "If it was only that simple."

She'd just screwed her lens cap on her camera when his mother arrived at the corral. Bridget managed to bestow a bright smile on the older woman. "It's good seeing you again. Well, I'm off."

"Don't run off on my account," Joan Gentry said. "I've been trying to call you all day," she told Josh. "I should have known you'd be out here. I wanted to remind you of your father's birthday on Sunday. He's sixty, so we're having a party."

"A party," Josh said scowling at Bridget. Bridget knew what it meant. He wanted her to go now, to leave before something awful happened like his mother inviting her to the party too. She shifted from one foot to the other. But she couldn't just leave. His mother might think she was rude when she'd told her not to run off.

"Yes, nothing extravagant. He wouldn't like that. But the whole family will be there, Lauren, Martha and the boys. And some neighbors. Will you still be in town, Bridget?"

"Me? Oh, I don't think... I mean my plans are up in the air."

"Because we'd love to have you join us, wouldn't we Josh?"

"We'd love it," he said

"Well, in that case," Bridget said, as if she hadn't recognized the sarcasm in his tone. He glared at her. His discomfort was so apparent she almost laughed. To repay him for kissing her and then apologizing, for lighting her fire and then dousing it before it had a chance to burn, she told his mother she'd be delighted to come to the birthday party. Then she took her camera and left. She knew he was watching her. She felt the heat of his gaze as she walked down the path to the barn and all the way to her car. She knew she'd annoyed him. That was nothing compared to what he'd done to her.

He'd unleashed the passion deep inside her she hadn't known existed. He'd made her feel, and made her want what she couldn't have. Him. And there was nothing she could do about it; he'd made that quite clear. She was beginning to regret having accepted his mother's invitation. How awkward was it going to be, seeing him surrounded by his family? Would they guess something was going on between them by the way he would studiously ignore her? Would they know how much she was attracted to Josh? And would they feel sorry for her because they knew she hadn't a hope in hell of attracting him?

Two long days went by. She sent the film, and the pictures absolutely wowed the Wild Mustang people, according to Kate. They weren't out of focus and they weren't overexposed. But they did need some video footage of possible settings on the ranch. Bridget stepped out of the phone booth on Main Street after a long conversation with Kate and looked up the street.

There wasn't much to see, a few wranglers sitting on a bench in front of the general store, a truckload of hay slowly lumbering down the street. The waitress from the diner standing in front of the bank, waiting for it to open. Then she thought about the noise, the traffic, the smog in the city. She thought of how Tally and Suzy had been friends since high school and would probably stay friends along with the others in their class for years. Her friends in the city were friends from work, likely to move or be transferred at any time.

Just then Suzy came walking down the street in her direction waving to get her attention.

"I just wanted to tell you I'm having a party," she said. "A week from Saturday. I hope you can come. After we met you, I got to thinking about Josh and everything. Tally and I decided we'd failed him. We'd let him bury himself on his ranch. So I decided to take the bull by the horns, or whatever, and get the old gang together again. What's left of us, that is. You'll still be here, won't you?" she asked anxiously.

"Probably." Bridget said. "But I'm not part of the gang."

"You will be. Everyone's dying to meet you."

Bridget smiled. "That's nice. What can I bring?"

"Just yourself. We'll have a barbecue outside, because my house is really small, but my yard is big. Big enough for a volleyball net. I live in town. You can walk there from here."

Bridget wanted to ask if Josh was coming, but she was afraid to act too interested.

"The amazing thing is that I talked Josh into coming," Suzy said. "I must be more persuasive than I thought."

A flutter of butterflies stirred in Bridget's stomach. What had Suzy said to convince Josh to come? One thing she knew for sure. She hadn't told him she intended to invite Bridget, or the answer would have been a resounding no.

"You didn't mention the cologne commercial, did you?" Bridget asked.

"No, I don't think I did. But he knows I know. I mean, what's the big secret? I did mention meeting you. And I told him I'd ask you to the party, too. Just as an added incentive."

Incentive? If she only knew. "And he didn't back out?" she asked.

"Of course not. Why should he?"

He might be afraid she'd attack him again. "No reason. Well, it was good to see you again," Bridget said. Then she went to her room and loaded her minicam. She had to go to the ranch, but she was afraid to. How was she going to avoid Josh if she was taking pictures of his ranch?

Settings, she reminded herself. Just settings. She didn't need him in the settings. And if she saw him she'd be cool and self-contained. She'd look at him with calm detachment and not let herself be swept off her feet. But first she'd call and tell him she was coming. Then he could be as prepared as she was.

Max answered the phone. He said his dad was outside someplace. He said Bridget should come out right away, because he had things to show her.

She smiled to herself. If it weren't for Josh, she'd feel positively welcome in this town. Everyone else seemed to find her an agreeable addition. Except for him. He was no doubt counting the days until she left.

Max met her at the gate to the ranch on his bicycle.

"Are you...are you alone?" she asked him after she'd parked her car in the driveway.

"My dad's out that way." He waved his hand in a westerly direction. "He's got his phone with him so I can call if there's a 'mergency. I told him you were coming. Said he'll be home for lunch."

She decided she'd be gone by then.

"First come and see my pet rat," Max said.

She gave a little shudder. "A rat?"

"He's white. Grandma doesn't like him, but he's real friendly."

"Is he in a cage?" Bridget asked anxiously as she followed Max down the hall to his bedroom.

"Yeah, but I can take him out and let you hold him."

"Really? I don't know if I'm ready for that, Max."

Max wove his way through his collection of miniature cars and trucks spread out on the floor of his room, motioning Bridget to follow him to the bookcase where the rat resided in a large wood and mesh cage lined with fresh wood shavings. There was an automatic water spout in one corner and some lettuce in a dish. Someone cared for this rat, that much was obvious.

"Wake up, Barney," Max said. Obediently the rat came out of his empty soup can, blinked in the bright daylight, then stood on his back legs and looked out at them, his whiskers twitching.

Max unlatched the cover and picked up the rat. "Wanna hold him?" he asked Bridget.

Bridget swallowed hard. She looked at the rat. It *was* cute. Kind of. But still a rat. She reached out with one finger and touched its fur. It was soft. It wasn't so bad. She looked into its beady eyes. Max took that to be a *yes*. He set the rat in her open palm. She bit her lip, but held her hand steady. The seconds dragged by. "Okay, that's enough for today," she said.

Max nodded and put Barney back in his cage. He beamed his approval at Bridget's courage. Then they went outside. While Bridget got her camcorder from her car,

Max went to get his bike. She knelt on the grass and focused her camera while Max came racing down the driveway wearing his helmet and doing wheelies. She smiled, knowing that Josh was nowhere in the vicinity and wouldn't be back until lunchtime. It was good to know he was just as anxious to avoid her as she was to avoid him.

From wheelies Max progressed to riding no-handed, grinning impudently at the camera. After each trick Max performed, Bridget cheered loudly, which encouraged him to try even harder. She would have clapped, but she had both hands on the recorder. He finally screeched to a halt in front of her, red-cheeked and out of breath. When she showed him what she'd recorded through her viewfinder, he laughed uproariously and begged her to let him watch it again and again.

"That's enough, Max," she said. "I'll leave the cassette with you, and you can keep it and watch it whenever you want to. You have a VCR, don't you?"

He nodded. "That's cool. Thanks, Bridget," he said, remembering his manners. "Now it's your turn. You do something. I'll take your picture."

She hesitated only a moment. It was an expensive machine, but it would be a good lesson for him in responsibility. "Okay, come here." She knelt next to him and looped the strap over his neck, then showed him where to squeeze the trigger. "Now don't bump the lens and try to hold the camera steady. Is it too heavy for you?"

He held the camera up to his eyes. "Huh-uh. It's funny. It's just like a slingshot. You aim and you shoot, right?"

"Right," she said.

"Go ahead, do something," he said.

She looked around, suddenly self-conscious.

"Do a somersault. There on the grass." He pointed to a level grassy area.

She shrugged. Why not? No one was there. She sat

down, tucked her legs under her and rolled over. "How was that?" she asked, picking the grass out of her hair.

"Good. This is neat. I want one of these kind of cameras."

She laughed. It felt good to roll around in the grass. To smell the air. To be in the company of a five-year-old whose only goal was to have a good time. "By the way," she said casually, looking over her shoulder. "You're sure your dad isn't around?"

He shook his head. "Nope. Why...do you want to take his picture?"

"No, not today. Today I have to take some pictures of the ranch."

"Not yet. I wanna take some more pictures of you. Do a dance, or something."

Reassured that Josh was nowhere in the vicinity, Bridget pirouetted around, kicking up her heels, skipping and hopping with crazy abandon, anything to make Max laugh. Which he did.

"Hey," she said, "you're jiggling the camera up and down. You have to hold it steady."

"I can't," he protested. "Not when I'm laughing."

She ran across the grass and picked him and the camera up and spun them around in her arms. "Stop," he yelled. "I'm the camera man. You can't pick up the camera man." His wheat-colored hair tickled her nose, and the camera bounced against her chest.

When he wriggled so much she had to put him down, she asked for the camera, but he didn't want to give it up. "I wanna do a whatcha-ma-call-it, where I get up real close." He pointed the camera at her face.

"Closeup," she said.

"Say a poem or sing a song," he instructed.

Bridget obliged by doing two children's songs, both with gestures. First she sang about a teapot, then about an eensy-weensy spider who climbed up the water spout. They were both a big hit with Max.

They watched the video together through the viewfinder, their heads side by side, then she gave him the cassette and put a fresh one into her camcorder.

"Now I have to get to work," she said, slinging her camcorder over her shoulder. "I need to take pictures of some outdoor places, like the corral or the pasture."

"Can I come?"

"Sure, you can show me the best spots." He could also protect her from his father, she thought.

But there was no need. He was nowhere in sight. They climbed to the top of the rise behind the barn. They trudged through the stand of fir trees. They circled the outside of the corral, taking pictures of everything. But they never saw Josh. Not all morning. Not that she wanted to. She left before noon. In plenty of time. Max was back on his bike as she got into her car, doing jumps off a wooden platform he'd set up. She was glad to see him wearing a helmet, a new addition since his run-in with her that first day.

She gave a wistful glance in the rearview mirror. Nobody'd ever told her that five-year-old boys were so much fun. If she'd known that, maybe she would have tried a little harder to find a husband. If she were Max's mother, she'd be inside right now, making peanut butter sandwiches, or whatever five-going-on-six-year-olds ate, while she watched proudly from the kitchen window as he performed outside. Then Josh would come home for lunch, and they'd sit around the table, with the sun streaming in the window and talk about nothing...and everything.

What was wrong with her? Why didn't she dream about marrying a movie star or winning the lottery? Either one was more likely to happen than living happily ever after with the most confirmed bachelor in the entire state of Nevada.

She didn't have enough to do, that was her problem. That was the reason for these erratic thoughts. Who said she wanted to get married, anyhow? Who would want a ready-made family? Who would want to be a stepmother with all the grief that entailed? Who would give up a promising career to spend the rest of their life in some small town nobody'd ever heard of instead of a big city where she could be Somebody? She bit her lip to keep from calling out the answer. *She would.*

If she hadn't been sitting in her car daydreaming instead of driving out of the ranch, she would have missed Josh. But suddenly there he was in her rearview mirror, galloping toward her on a wild mustang. If she'd been smart she would have put her car in gear and driven away as fast as she could, but now it was too late. The hoofbeats of his horse rang through the dry air. Closer and closer he came until he filled her mirror, her mind and her thoughts. Now he would think she'd come to see him. He would think she couldn't wait until his father's birthday party, she had to come out here today.

"Where are you going?" he called as he pulled up alongside of her and swung out of his saddle. His hair was matted to his head, beads of sweat dripped off his forehead, and his dirty jeans were molded to his legs. She wondered for the hundredth time what made her heart thud wildly every time she saw him. What made her hands shake so much she had to grip the steering wheel so he wouldn't notice. He was handsome, yes. But so were many other men. He was rugged, he was strong and he was good at what he did. He was also sexy. So? So were lots of other men. It was more than that. So much more.

"Going? Going back to town. I was just, you know, taking some pictures," she said. "I didn't want to disturb you again, so—"

"So you snuck in here while I wasn't looking."

"I didn't sneak. I drove in. I took some pictures. Max showed me around and was very helpful."

"Didn't it occur to you that you should wait for me?" He braced his arms against her car and leaned forward until his sun-bronzed face was framed in her open window. Oh, Lord, this was just what she'd wanted to avoid. Another encounter. Of the closest kind. The kind where the male, musky scent of his body filled her senses. The kind where she couldn't get enough breath in her lungs to breathe. Why hadn't she left ten minutes ago? Five?

She took a deep breath. "No," she said, "it didn't. I thought it would be best if we avoided any more—"

"Awkward situations?"

She nodded. She couldn't have said it better herself.

"I told you it wouldn't happen again. Don't you trust me?"

"Yes, of course." It's me I don't trust, she admitted to herself.

"What have you been doing with yourself? You must be bored out of your mind, hanging around Harmony."

She managed a cool smile. "Not at all. I have my camera. There's lots to take pictures of. Being from here, you probably don't see the beauty of the landscape. But I see it through a stranger's eyes."

"Is that right?" he asked, skepticism lacing his voice. "By the way, don't feel you have to come to my father's birthday party. It won't be anything exciting. Just family."

"I don't know what makes you think I need constant excitement, that I'm bored if I'm not in the middle of Union Square. I'm perfectly capable of amusing myself anywhere. As for the party, I said I'd come and I will. I'm looking forward to it. I don't have a big family. In fact there's just two of us left, my dad and I. And I don't think I've ever given him a birthday party. Your mother was kind enough to invite me and...and I'm coming." Just knowing he didn't want her there made her determined that even wild horses couldn't keep her away.

"Suit yourself," he said.

"Yes, I'll do that."

There was a long silence. She stared straight ahead through the windshield. She could feel Josh's eyes on her, tracing the outline of her cheek; feeling the heat of his gaze as it lingered on her eyelids, then her lips. His fingers rested on the edge of the open window. Then he raised one hand and plucked a blade of grass from behind her ear. Her skin burned where he touched her. Next he stroked the outline of her cheek with one broad finger. Her heart pounded. She had to get out of there. All she had to do was insert the key in the ignition, but she missed. Her car keys rattled. Her nerves rattled more. But at least they were silent.

Why didn't he just get back on his horse and ride away? Or was he waiting for her to make the first move.

"Well," she said, "I'd better be getting back to town."

"What for?" he asked.

"Lunch." She looked at her watch. "It's lunchtime."

"Who are you having lunch with?" Josh could just picture all those randy cowboys who hung out at the diner putting the moves on the attractive newcomer.

"Do you care?"

"Well, you're new in town. There are men who would take advantage of a pretty stranger."

"A pretty stranger. That's the nicest thing you've said about me since I got here. You've done everything but have me run out of town."

"How can you say that?" he said with a flicker of amusement in his eyes. "You misunderstood me. That's just our way here in Harmony. You'll get used to it. If you're around long enough," he added in an undertone.

"I'll be around long enough to get the film footage I

want, I assure you," she said, meeting his cool blue gaze. "And after that I'll be out of your hair."

With a firm grasp on the car keys, Bridget finally turned on the ignition. Josh took a step away from her car, and she tore out of his driveway without a backward glance while she still had the last word. Not an easy thing to accomplish in his company.

"What did you and Bridget do this morning?" Josh asked Max across the lunch table as they ate a bowl of canned soup together.

"Some stuff. Wait till you see what I got. A movie of me and Bridget."

"A movie?"

"Yeah, I made it, too. The part about her. She showed me how. She made the part about me." He pulled the cassette out of his pocket and waved it in front of his father. "Wanna see it?"

"Sure." Josh took the cassette and held it between his thumb and forefinger as if he was afraid it would burn him. He didn't want to see it. He didn't want to see any pictures of Bridget. "Did Bridget really come all the way out here just to take pictures of you and her?"

"I dunno. I guess so. No, wait. She wanted to take pictures of outdoor stuff, so I showed her the best places. I told her you'd be back for lunch but she quick got in her car."

"I saw her," he said, wondering why he'd made such an effort to catch her before she left, when she had such an unsettling effect on him. "We'll watch the video tonight," he promised. "After dinner. You're going to Nathan Hogan's to play this afternoon. Did you forget?"

Max hadn't forgotten and went to find his baseball cards to trade with his friend. Josh drove him there, then came back and tried once again to saddle his newest horse. It was the most demanding job he could think of, the one most likely to take his concentration away from that woman who wouldn't leave him alone. It was bad enough she had to spend the morning at his ranch with his son, but she had to leave behind a video recording that he could watch.

He could watch it now if he wanted to. The cassette was on top of their VCR in the den, tempting him to have a look. But he didn't want to. Besides he'd told Max they'd watch it tonight. He glanced at his watch. Still three hours until he could pick up Max. Longer until they could watch the damned video.

He blamed this distraction on his being alone too much for too long. That was why he agreed to go to Suzy's party. His mother was right, he needed to get out and see some other people. Then he would realize that Bridget was just an ordinary woman...with ordinary long, smooth legs and ordinary warm, hazel eyes the color of autumn leaves, skin as soft as rose petals. His fingers still prickled where he'd touched her hair, where he'd stroked her cheek. He hadn't meant to. He hadn't meant to have anything to do with the woman. What happened? What went wrong? Because before he realized it, she was coming to his father's birthday party as well as the party at Suzy's.

He hadn't been to a party for years. He and Molly didn't go to parties. She was too busy doing good works. And he didn't care about socializing, though in high school he'd had a lot of friends. Somehow he'd drifted away from his old friends. That was what happened when you got married, you had different interests, different priorities.

Somehow the afternoon dragged by. He picked up Max from his friend's house. They ate dinner.

"Now, Dad, now," Max said, leaving his favorite fried-chicken TV dinner mostly untouched. "You gotta watch my movie." He dragged Josh by the hand into the pine-paneled den, where Max put on the video. They sat together

on the couch, Max squirming and wiggling and jumping
up to put his finger on the image on the screen in case Josh
missed anything. Josh didn't miss a thing. He watched mes-
merized, laughing hard at Bridget's eensy-weensy spider
song, so hard that Max gave him a wide-eyed look and
asked him if he was okay. It made him realize that he didn't
laugh very often. Not anymore.

He sat there watching Max and Bridget perform over and
over again. Even after Max lost interest and went off to his
room to look at his new baseball cards, Josh continued to
watch Bridget do her somersault and sing and dance on the
grass. She was so…so sweetly uninhibited. So delightfully,
wonderfully charming. He'd never seen her that way, so
loose, so natural, unreserved except…for that day when
she'd wrapped her legs around his waist and kissed him
like he'd never been kissed before. Aroused him in a way
that had set his body on fire; even now it continued to
smolder. He knew he had to put out the flames. That was
why he'd been avoiding Bridget. He was afraid that the fire
would flare up all over again and he'd never be able to put
it out.

That was why he was watching her on the screen. She
couldn't cause any damage to his psyche that way. She
couldn't penetrate his defenses. She was harmless. He
could turn her off anytime he wanted. The problem was,
he didn't want to. He wanted to keep watching. And he
did.

He finally roused himself, turned off the VCR and put
Max to bed. If only he could sleep as soundly as a five-
year-old, he thought, watching him enviously from the
doorway. If his dreams weren't so disturbingly full of
Bridget, maybe he could.

Chapter Five

It was a beautiful day for a birthday party. The sky was cloudless, the air was warm and dry. There was no reason to be nervous. No reason for Bridget's stomach to churn like an egg beater, just because she was going to meet his family and friends, and just because she had to tell him that the film crew would arrive sometime this week and had to ask him where they could stay—that was no reason to panic. She imagined his dour expression, his refusal to cooperate, to pose for any pictures or to let them stay on the property. Josh's mother greeted Bridget at the front door of the sprawling ranch house by taking both hands in hers. She hoped his mother didn't notice how her fingers were ice cold.

"The men are skeet shooting in the pasture," his mother said. "The kids are playing behind the house, and the women are in the kitchen as usual. Come on in and meet everybody."

The spacious kitchen was full of women, wearing everything from jeans to shorts to cotton sundresses. Bridget had a hard time remembering their names, but they had no trouble remembering hers, since they'd heard all about her and the Wild Mustang account. She was glad Josh wasn't there to hear them exclaim about how exciting it was that Josh was going to be a big star. She could just hear him now. "I don't wear cologne, nobody I know wears cologne, and I wouldn't want to know anybody who wears it. Have you ever smelled a wild mustang? Would you want to smell like one?"

"How did you hear about Josh?" his sister Lauren asked, interrupting her thoughts, as she mixed some dough for biscuits.

"Did you hold tryouts for the part of the Wild Mustang Man?" his sister Martha asked, wiping her hands on an apron.

Bridget joined her at the counter to help tear lettuce for the salad. "Oh, no. The first day I came to town I had coffee in the diner and I asked who was the best trainer of wild mustangs. I got a list, and his name was on top. I came out to the ranch and saw him ride. I knew he was the one."

"Did you hear that, Martha?" his mother said proudly. "She knew he was the one."

"But did *he* know he was the one?" his sister Martha asked. "I can't believe he said he'd do it. It's not like Josh to want to be in the spotlight."

Bridget frowned, thinking back to the day at the wild horse roundup, when Josh had stormed over to where she was talking to that wrangler, grabbed her by the arm and told her he'd do it.

"It may be the money," she said. But she didn't really believe it was. From what she knew of him, he wasn't motivated by money. "Being a spokesman for a product can be lucrative."

"Spokesman?" Lauren said. "Is he going to speak?

Bridget smiled. "No. Oh, no. He just has to ride a wild mustang."

"Then why is he so upset about it?" Lauren asked.

Bridget's face fell. Why *was* he so upset about it? Was he still embarrassed to be connected to a men's cologne? Or was he embarrassed to be connected to her in any way?

"You know Josh," Martha said. "All he ever wanted was to live a simple life. Home and hearth and all that. Now he's being dragged into the spotlight."

"Not really," Bridget said. "The way I picture it, the logo has the outline of a man on a horse outlined against the western sky." She'd never forget her first glimpse of him on that hill and how her heart pounded knowing she'd found him. On her first try. "No one will see his face. No one will know who he is."

"But we'll know," his sister said. "Everyone in Harmony will know."

"I guess so," Bridget said. "I hope he doesn't think *I* told everyone."

"Of course not. You don't know anyone to tell. What do you think of Harmony, anyway?" Lauren asked. "I could hardly wait to leave. Isn't it the most boring place in the world?"

"Actually…people are really friendly here. That's what impresses me. The waitress in the diner knows my name, and two women stopped and introduced themselves to me and invited me to a party next week. And the air is so clear, you can see for miles."

Lauren smiled at her mother. "Looks like we've got a convert here. She sounds like the chamber of commerce, if there was one. Do you ride, hunt or fish?"

"No, but Max is teaching me to shoot a slingshot," Bridget said.

"He would. Josh ought to teach you to ride while you're here," his sister suggested.

"Those mustangs look pretty wild to me." Wouldn't Josh just love to give her horseback riding lessons? She could just picture the look on his face as he stopped his work to teach her to ride.

"He has other horses," his sister said. "Gentle horses."

"Besides, he seems pretty busy," Bridget said.

"That's an act," Martha confided to her. "It gives him an excuse not to do anything but work. He buries himself so can't socialize. Ever since Molly died. Tells himself he doesn't have time. But he does."

"Tell us about yourself," Lauren said. "Are you married? Do you have a family?"

"I'm not married. I was engaged last year, but I'm not anymore. I've been told I spend too much time working. Just like Josh. But I have a new business. So I need to devote myself to it if I want to succeed."

"And you *do* want to succeed."

"Oh, yes." How to explain the burning desire to show people she could make a go of it. To show one person in particular—the man who dumped her and got her fired and told her she couldn't do it. Couldn't do anything.

"But I envy you your big family," Bridget said wistfully, looking around the kitchen. "I'm an only child. My mother died a few years ago and my father retired to Southern California. He's in great shape, though, still runs every day. Makes me look like a wimp."

"You don't look like a wimp to me," Josh's mother said with a warm smile. "In fact, Max told me you actually held his pet rat. That's not something a wimp would do."

"He's a very persuasive little boy," she said. "I'm afraid he'll have me doing wheelies down the driveway before I know it—even though I don't know how to ride a bike."

"He needs a mother," Martha said softly.

"Don't let Josh hear you say that," her sister said. "He's not going to replace Molly."

"I didn't say he should replace Molly. Nobody can replace her. Nobody could even try. But he's only what, thirty-two? He's got a lot of good years left. What's he going to do with them?" Martha asked. "Besides train horses."

"Who's he supposed to marry?" Lauren asked, while Bridget sliced cucumbers and waited breathlessly for the answer. Who *was* he supposed to marry?

Martha shook her head. "There's nobody left in Harmony. They all got married out of high school or left town like we did. We'd have to import somebody."

"Now, girls," their mother said. "Josh is capable of finding someone on his own. When the time is right."

There was a long silence. Bridget sliced faster, hoping they weren't looking at her. Wondering if she— No, she'd made it clear she was married to her job. A job she loved. A job she was excited about. And *he'd* made it clear she was the *last* person he'd ever marry.

"Bridget," his mother said. "Would you mind taking the steaks out to my husband at the barbecue? It's time we got started."

Bridget was relieved to get outside, to let the air cool her heated cheeks as she rounded the back of the house with the platter in her hands. The conversation was getting a little too sticky for her. They talked to her and in front of her as if she was a part of the family. As if she cared as much as they did about Josh and Max and the imaginary woman who was missing from their lives.

When in fact, as much as she liked both Josh and his son, she was just a temporary diversion. For both of them. She followed the smell of charcoal to the huge homemade barbecue stand. Behind the billowing smoke Josh and an older man, who looked very much like him, stood fanning the flames.

"Here we are," the older man said, reaching for the platter of meat.

Josh dropped his tongs and looked at her as if he wondered what she was doing there. He must have forgotten she'd been invited. He didn't speak until his father jabbed him in the ribs.

"Bridget, meet my dad. Dad, this is the lady from the ad agency."

"Oh," his father said. "So this is her. You didn't tell me she was so pretty."

"No, but I'm sure Max did. Max is very fond of Bridget," Josh said. The emphasis was on the word *Max*. Bridget knew he didn't want anyone to think he was the least bit fond of Bridget. He considered her a necessary evil, a nuisance and a temptation who made him feel guilty.

"I can understand why. How do you like our little town so far?" his father asked.

"Very much. Everyone is so friendly." Everyone but your son, she thought.

"Bought yourself a wild mustang yet?" he asked.

"Not yet. I'm afraid I'd have no place to keep it in my apartment in San Francisco."

"Real problem getting them into the elevator," he said. "San Francisco? Wonderful town. The wife is taking me there this week for my birthday present. Supposed to be a surprise, but I found out about it. We're leaving in the morning."

"I didn't know that," Josh said. "I'll feed your horses for you."

His father nodded, then cupped his ear toward the house. "Your mother's calling me," he said, lifting his apron off over his head and handing it to Bridget. "Do you mind taking over for me?"

Before she could protest that she didn't know how to

barbecue steaks, and she didn't want to be stuck alone with Josh, he was gone, jogging toward the house.

She took his father's place, wearing his apron and standing next to Josh. She tapped the long, two-pronged fork against the grill, not wanting to broach the subject of the film crew, not yet. Finally they both spoke at once.

"Your family is very nice."

"I understand you like rats."

They turned to face each other. If she didn't know better she would have sworn he almost smiled. At her.

"I'm terrified of rats," she confessed.

"That's not what I heard."

"I guess I put up a pretty good front. I didn't want to hurt his feelings."

"Whose? The rat's?" Josh asked.

"I understand they can tell if you don't like them," Bridget said.

"Like kids and horses," he said.

"Both good judges of character," she said

"So they say." He threw a steak on the grill. Then another. "Having a good time?" he asked, with a sideways glance in her direction.

"I was."

"You can go back to the kitchen if you want. I can handle this by myself."

"It's nice to be outside," she said lightly.

"Then why don't you make yourself useful?"

She speared a piece of meat and tossed it on her side of the grill. "Like that?"

He didn't answer. But she knew he was watching her out of the corner of his eye. "Do you like parties?" he asked.

"Not usually. I'm shy and…"

"You're shy? You came barging into my house and bled all over my bathroom. I'd hate to see you if you weren't shy. What would you have done, raided the refrigerator, rolled up the rugs and done a dance?''

"I don't dance."

"No? What was that you were doing on my lawn?'' There was a note of amusement in his voice.

"Me, on your lawn?"

"Don't deny it. I have the blade of grass to prove it. And the video.''

"Oh, Lord." Her face flamed. "I didn't know you were going to watch it. That was for Max.''

"Oh, yes, I watched it. Max insisted. I had no choice.'' He chuckled. She tossed a quick glance in his direction. Yes, he was smiling. His mouth was turned up at the corners. Crinkly lines branched from the corners of his eyes The worry lines in his forehead were gone. He was even better looking than she'd first thought. And that was saying something. "It was more interesting than anything on our cable TV station," he added.

Now was the time, she thought. To tell him when the crew was arriving. While he was in a good mood. But before she could speak, a line of guests began to form in front of the barbecue. Plates in hand, they were laughing and talking and teasing Josh.

"Hey, Josh, what's that I smell? Some kind of mustang cologne?'' his brother-in-law asked, holding his nose.

"You want a steak in your face, Ray?'' Josh asked with a menacing growl. "See what I told you?'' he said to Bridget under his breath. "I'm the laughing stock.'' But he didn't sound too upset.

When Max came by, the boy grinned at Bridget, but he didn't take any meat. "I'm not hungry," he told his dad.

"He looks a little pale," Bridget noted, watching him with a little frown.

"Just excited," Josh explained. "All his cousins are here today."

"Hmm," she said, watching him follow two bigger boys to a picnic table under a tree, marching along, trying to keep up.

After all the guests were served, Bridget took a steak, baked beans and potato salad and sat down at a long picnic table to eat. In a few minutes Josh sat down across from her and introduced her to everyone at the table. If he'd wanted to avoid her, there were other tables, other places to sit. She sent him a grateful look across the table. He didn't notice. He was shaking some steak sauce on his plate, acting as though introducing her to his friends and relatives was the most normal thing in the world to do. But the normal thing for him would have been to ignore her, pretend she wasn't there.

A leather-faced rancher turned to Bridget. "So, what do you think of the wild mustangs?"

Bridget took a deep breath. At least he hadn't asked what she thought of Harmony.

"They're beautiful. They seem to be living symbols of the Old West. Just watching them makes me feel like I'm part of the pioneer spirit," Bridget said, borrowing a few key words from the Wild Free-Roaming Horse Act of 1971.

"Well said." The rancher smiled broadly. Then he turned to Josh. "How you coming with that buckskin you've been working with?"

Josh hesitated a moment. What could he say? That he'd been so distracted by the woman sitting across the table from him he hadn't been able to concentrate on breaking his horse? "Coming along," he said. "Slowly. I've had some distractions." He stared at her, so she would have no doubt he meant her. When she met his gaze, her cheeks turned as red as wild poppies. She turned her attention to the food on her plate, but he kept his eyes on her. And suddenly he realized how much fun he was having at this party he'd been dreading. And part of it was due to Bridget. No, all of it was due to her.

Her presence heightened his awareness of the warm sun, the smell of succulent meat cooking on the grill, the friendly laughter around the table. He was seeing everything through a stranger's eyes. Her eyes. And appreciating everything he'd taken for granted. Because of her.

After lunch his brother-in-law organized a game of horseshoes. He asked Bridget if she wanted to play. She agreed, but there were questions in her eyes. He knew what they were. What's going on here? I thought you didn't want me around. How come you're being so nice?

How come? Damned if he knew. He only knew he was intensely aware of her, of the curve of her cheek, the sunlight in her hair, the glow of her eyes, the way she blushed, the lilt of her voice, every expression that crossed her face, every word she spoke. He didn't want her out of his sight for fear he'd miss something.

He remembered the heated kisses they'd shared the other day, the warmth of her body and how she'd promised to keep her hands off him. He also remembered the guilt he'd felt afterward. But he didn't feel it now. There was no reason to feel guilty. He was just being hospitable to a guest. Yeah, sure.

"But I don't know how to throw horseshoes," she protested as they walked across the field.

"Nothing to it."

"Is it anything like operating a slingshot?"

"Same thing. Pull back, aim and let go. I'll help you."

He found that to help her it was necessary to be on her team. To wrap his arms around her. It was essential that her silky hair brush his cheek, that she fit in his arms like she was meant to be there. Working together, with his hand holding on to hers, holding the horseshoe, they won a few points. They also won the attention of several other guests.

"Foul play," his sister yelled from the other end of the pit. "Two against one. I don't have a chance."

Bridget tried to pull out of his arms, but he tightened his grasp around her. "She's a sore loser," he explained just loud enough for Martha to hear.

When the game was over and his father took a seat in the middle of the crowd to open his presents, Josh's sister sidled up to him where he was leaning against the cotton-wood tree.

"What's going on?" she asked under her breath.

"Going on?" he repeated innocently.

She punched him in the arm. "Don't play games with me. Do you think I'm blind? Do you think I've been married so long I don't recognize out-and-out flirting when I see it?"

"That's all it is," he said, suddenly serious. "I would never— You know I'd never get serious about anyone again."

"Why not? You're free, you're over twenty-one, and you've got a lot to offer the right woman."

"The right woman was Molly. And despite the fact that we had everything going for us—"

"She died. But you didn't die with her. You're alive, Josh. And so is this woman you brought to the party. She's delightful. She's charming and if I'm not mistaken..."

"But you are mistaken. You're mistaken if you think I'd ever take a chance on love again. No matter how delightful and charming Bridget is."

"So you admit it," his sister said with a knowing smile.

"She's delightful and charming, and she's a career woman from the city. Do you think for one minute—"

"Yes, I do. I think if you gave her the time of day, she'd jump at the chance to give the country a try. I saw the way she looked around Mom's kitchen. She even said she envied our family."

"She did?"

"She did," his sister said. "You take it all for granted. But to a city girl, it can look pretty idyllic. Can't you see that?"

He shook his head.

"If you won't think of yourself, think about Max, about how he needs a mother."

"You're not the first person to tell me that. But I'm not going to marry someone so Max can have a mother. I'd only get married again if I fell in love. Which I'm not going to do," he added firmly.

"Oh, Josh," Martha said, her eyes filling with tears. "I just want you to be happy. Ever since you were a little kid, even from the day they brought you home from the hospital, Lauren and I have watched you as you grew up, proud of what you did, envying you your skill at making friends, playing football, taming horses. It seemed like there was nothing you couldn't do, nothing you couldn't succeed at. I can't stand to think of you growing old alone."

Touched at her concern, Josh gave her a brief hug. "I'm not going to be alone," he teased. "I'm going to come and live with you and Ray."

She shook her head and smiled through her unshed tears. "Okay. I've said my piece. I know it's none of my business, so I'll shut up now. But if I were you…" He saw her look across the lawn to where Bridget was sitting cross-legged on the ground next to Max.

"I get the message," he said quickly. He felt torn up inside. As if the emotions he'd kept under wraps these past two years had been stirred up, and he was left feeling unsure of how he really felt. About anything.

From his spot under the tree, he watched his father open his presents. Bridget gave him a silver belt buckle she'd bought at the general store in town. His father was surprised and tickled.

"You didn't have to do that," his father told her, holding it up for everyone to see. Josh could tell how pleased he was by the glint in his eye and the way his father glanced pointedly at him as if he was saying, Look, did you see that? See what she gave me? See how well she fits in?

His sisters left early with their families for the long drive back to Reno. Nothing more was said about his future, but Martha, always the emotional one, hugged him tightly before she left. Other guests made jokes on their way out the door about his being the Wild Mustang Man. It didn't bother him the way he thought it would. In fact, some of the jokes were downright funny. By evening he realized he'd laughed more that day than he had in two years.

He said goodbye to his parents and got last-minute instructions on caring for their animals while they were in San Francisco that week. Then he looked for Bridget. She was out at the driveway with Max, kneeling next to him, with her hand on his forehead.

She looked up when she heard Josh approach. "His head is so warm. I wonder if he has a fever."

Josh ran to his side and lifted Max into his arms. His son felt warm all over. Max was never sick. Maybe a cold or a sore throat, but nothing like this. Oh, God, don't let him be sick, he prayed. He carried Max to his truck and set him in the front seat. His head drooped. His chin hit his chest. He slouched over in the seat, unable to sit up straight. "I'll get him home to bed, take his temperature and call the doc if necessary," Josh told her, trying to sound like he wasn't scared out of his mind.

Then he leaped into the driver's seat and drove home, his palms sweaty against the steering wheel. He watched Max out of the corner of his eye, gripping the steering wheel so tightly his knuckles turned white. He forced himself to stay calm, telling himself Max would be okay. But the memories came flooding back of that day two years ago when his life fell apart.

He got the boy undressed, sponged the dirt off his face and put him to bed. His temperature was 102. Not high for a child. But all he could think of was Molly. This was how it started, with a moderate fever. Then it rose and rose. And in a few days the galloping virus had taken her life. In the days, weeks and months that had followed, he'd dreaded getting out of bed in the morning. If it hadn't been for Max, if Max hadn't needed him, he would have stayed in bed, hiding from the world. Max was all he had left. If he lost his son as well as his wife he wouldn't want to live.

"Dad," Max said hoarsely, trying to sit up. "Would you feed Barney for me?"

Josh's throat tightened painfully as he assured him he would. Imagine a five-year-old thinking about his pet when he couldn't even hold his head up. He gave Max a drink of water, tucked him in and went downstairs to call the doctor and leave a message for him.

As long as he was busy, feeding the rat, making the phone call, Josh was okay. But standing there in Max's room, watching him toss and turn, his heart ached with worry and apprehension. He clenched his hands into fists, vowing nothing bad would happen to his son.

After an eternity of waiting, the doctor finally called around midnight, explaining he'd been out delivering a baby in the next county. When Josh described Max's symptoms, the doctor told him to observe him and call in the morning.

"Keep the fluids going. Make him comfortable. Children's ibuprofen would be okay. But it's probably nothing."

Nothing. It was probably nothing, Josh told himself over and over. But he didn't believe it. He couldn't sleep. He sat next to Max's bed all night watching him sleep, listening to him mumble and thrash around.

In the morning Max's temperature had risen two degrees. His face was flushed and he was almost delirious. Josh gave him apple juice and a pill and called the doctor again.

"You've got to get out here. He's sick. Really sick."

"Now, Josh, I'll be out there as soon as I can. Any rash?"

"Rash? Why?"

"Check his chest?"

"Hold on."

Max's chest and stomach were covered with tiny red dots. He was scratching like mad. Josh ran back to the phone to report the news.

"Uh-huh. That's what I figured."

"What?"

"Chicken pox. It's going around."

"Oh, my God." Josh heaved a sigh of relief.

"You had 'em?"

"Yeah. It's all coming back to me. I was home from school for two weeks in second grade. I caught them from my sisters. And gave them to my best friend. Itched like the devil. Poor kid," he said thinking of Max being confined for any length of time. He'd hate it. "You'll come by, anyway?" he asked.

"Right. Just to be sure. I have another patient out your way. See you in a while."

Josh did everything but stand on his head to amuse Max and keep his mind off the itching. He read books, or rather the same book about a little girl with a big red dog, over and over. He played a board game, which he lost, then a card game called Go Fish, which he won. By ten o'clock he was exhausted. He'd had no sleep and hadn't fed his animals or his father's.

When the phone rang, he brought it into Max's room.

"I called to see how Max was," Bridget said.

Just the sound of her voice chased the cobwebs from his mind. Made him feel like he wasn't alone.

"He's got a temperature of 104. A rash all over his chest. And he's a bear to be around," he said, making a fierce face at Max who stuck out his tongue at his father. "The good news is the doctor thinks it's only chicken pox."

"Of course. I remember when I had them. The itching was terrible. Poor kid."

Josh smiled. "That's what I said. At first. Now that I've been entertaining him for the past three hours I'm changing that to poor me."

"Can I help?"

"Could you help? I couldn't ask you…"

"Is that Bridget?" Max asked. "Gimme the phone. I wanna talk to her."

Josh handed the phone to Max. "I'm sick. Can you come and see me?" he asked in a small weak voice.

Josh couldn't hear what she said, but he couldn't imagine her saying no. Max handed the phone back to his father, fell back onto the pillow and closed his eyes.

"I can come out right away, that is if you want me."

Did he want her? Did birds fly south in the winter? But it wasn't fair. Wasn't right to drag her into his problems. He should have said No thanks. He should have insisted he could handle it by himself. And he could. But he didn't want to.

"I want you," he said, his voice coming out hoarse and rough. He could blame his lack of willpower on his lack of sleep, or his concern about Max, or his need to have someone to share the burden. But it went deeper than that. How deep he didn't know. He only knew she was coming and that he was more relieved than he wanted to admit.

Chapter Six

The doctor came, confirmed Max had chicken pox, gave him some ointment to ease the itching and left. Max slept, while Josh paced back and forth in front of the living room window watching and waiting for Bridget. When he saw her car coming up the driveway, he threw the door open and went outside. She'd barely stopped her car when he was there, opening her car door for her, barely waiting for her to emerge before he'd crushed her to him.

He chalked it up to fatigue and worry. He was just so glad to see her. To hold her. To feel her heart beating, sure and steady. He wanted to kiss her, to mold her body to his, to give her whatever she wanted, to take whatever she would give. But there was Max. So before he lost his head completely, he gripped her shoulders and muttered hoarsely, "Thanks for coming."

She nodded, her eyes wide and startled, seemingly at a loss for words. Not like her. Not like her, at all. They went into the house, and she followed him silently down the hall to Max's room. They stood at his bedside, watching him sleep. He wanted to put his arm around her, to pull her hip next to his, press her shoulder against his. But he didn't. He kept his arms at his side. It wouldn't be right. Wouldn't be fair. Because what he wanted was someone to share his problems with, to worry with him, to tell him what he already knew. That Max was going to be okay.

She couldn't do that. It wasn't fair to ask her. She deserved more than that. She deserved someone to share the good times and not be dragged down into someone else's worries. She bent over and laid her hand on Max's forehead.

"Oh, my gosh," she said. "He's warm. How does he feel?"

"Uncomfortable. Itchy. Unhappy. He'll be glad to see you when he wakes up."

"I brought some stuff for him," she said setting a shopping bag on the floor next to his bed. "I'll wait here till he opens his eyes. Go ahead, take a break. Don't you have things to do?"

"Don't you?"

She shook her head. "The film crew was scheduled to come here this week, but when I heard about Max I postponed it."

"I'll go feed my horses, then, if you're sure you'll be all right."

Bridget nodded. She heard the back door close behind Josh, and she looked out Max's bedroom window to watch him stride purposefully across the field toward the barn. So tall, so strong, so sure of himself. And yet this morning when he took her in his arms, and she felt his heart beat against hers, she felt for the first time that she had something to offer him. She had a fleeting feeling that he needed her. It only lasted for a moment And it was only because Max was sick and he had to go outside to do his chores. She wished it was more than that. She wished she had something she could give him. Something besides sympathy, understanding and comfort. Those he would accept. But what about love? Would he accept love? Not from her.

Too restless to sit at Max's bedside and watch him sleep, she picked up a dozen toy cars from the floor and put them in a plastic container where they joined many other miniature cars and trucks. She stashed a pile of dirty T-shirts and blue jeans in a basket in his closet. Then she walked around the room, looking at the pictures Max had pinned to his bulletin board, crayon drawings he'd made of motorcycles, pictures he'd cut from magazines of dinosaurs and a photograph of him with his mother and father.

Bridget studied the photo, noting that Max's smile matched his mother's smile, and his blue eyes were the same color as his father's. She felt the warmth radiating from the picture and sensed their love for each other. Envy and longing filled her heart. And jealousy—a most unbecoming emotion. And despair. Would she ever be a part of a family like that? The answer was No, never.

She moved on to his bookcase. Peered into the rat's cage but didn't see Barney. She wasn't sure she wanted to look into his beady eyes. She knew she didn't want to feel his sharp little claws on her hand. Not this morning. Not before lunch. Under the cage were Max's books. Books about animals, books about monsters and goblins. Some books she remembered from her own childhood and some she didn't. She picked out one she'd always loved and sat down in the chair next to his bed to read his book.

"Bridget," he mumbled, startling her out of her reverie. In his excitement to see her he sat up too quickly, had a dizzy spell and fell back down on his pillow. "You came. I knew you'd come."

"How are you?" she asked, putting her arms around his feverish little body.

"I'm too hot," he complained, trying to push the blankets off his bed.

Gently she tucked them around him again. "I brought you something to drink." She reached in her bag for a can of ginger ale, popped it open, stuck a straw in it and handed it to him.

"The bubbles tickle my nose," he said after he'd taken a big gulp. She set the can on his bedside table. "I got chicken pox," he said proudly.

"I know. I had them once myself. When I was about your age."

"What did you look like?" he asked.

"I guess I looked pretty funny with red dots all over me, just like you."

"I mean what did you look like when you were a little girl?"

"Oh. Well, I had bangs, like this." She drew a straight line across her forehead. "And short hair, about to here." She pointed to her jawbone.

"But you didn't have a bike, did you?"

"No. We lived in the city, and there was no place for me to ride. Are you going to teach me to ride when you get well?"

"Yeah." He scratched his chest. "When am I gonna get well?"

"I don't know. Maybe a week or two." She held up the book she'd chosen. "How would you like me to read you a story?"

He shook his head. "I already heard that one."

"Okay, how about something else?" She reached into her shopping bag and brought out a white sock which she put on her hand. "I brought a friend with me."

"Looks like a sock."

"It is a sock, but I'm going to make a puppet out of it." She drew a red mouth and blue eyes with felt-tip pens, so it looked like the sock had a face. "Hi, little boy." she said moving her hand so it looked like the sock was talking.

He grabbed her hand and held it. "I'm not little," he told the sock.

"Sorry. *Big* boy. My name is Bridget." She bobbed the puppet's head. "I need a friend to play with."

She took out another sock and made a hand puppet for Max. He moved his hand around inside the sock.

"I got a lot of friends," he said, "but I don't got a mom."

"Me either," she said. "My mom's in heaven too, Max."

"Do you miss her?" he asked, laying his hand with the sock on it down on the bed.

"Yes, I do."

"Do you have a picture of her?"

"I don't have it with me. But sometime I'll show it to you."

"Did she look like you? People say I look like my mom."

Max didn't look up. Bridget didn't turn around, but she was suddenly aware that they weren't alone in the room. Josh was in the doorway, or just outside the door. She couldn't see him there, but she felt his presence just as surely as if he'd touched her with his hand.

"Do you remember your mom?" Max asked.

"Yes," Bridget said with a catch in her voice.

"I don't remember mine."

Bridget took the sock off her hand and soothed his brow with her hand. "I remember lots of things, but right now I'm remembering once when I was little and my mom took me to get my first pair of fancy shoes. I might have been about five or six. They were black patent-leather with one strap. Here." She drew a line across her foot. "Anyway, I loved those shoes so much. I felt like a princess in those shoes. I didn't want to take them off. I wanted to wear them home. But my mother said I might scuff them or something, so we carried them home in a box.''

Max's eyes drifted shut. His head fell back onto the pillow. "You're as beautiful as a princess, Bridget," he muttered, and then he fell asleep.

She sat on the edge of the bed and watched him sleep. Josh came up behind her and put his hand on the nape of her neck. Tremors went up and down her spine. She reached for his hand and held it tight, fighting back tears for a sick little boy who couldn't remember his mother.

Carefully, so as not to disturb Max, she got up off the bed.

When she met Josh's gaze, she saw such sadness there she wanted to tell him he was a good father, a great father. That he'd done a fantastic job with his son. That it was normal for Max to have a hard time remembering his mother. He'd been so young when she died. But she knew instinctively it was not her place to say these things.

She followed Josh silently down the stairs into the kitchen where he poured them each a cup of coffee. "Did you get anything done?" she asked lightly.

"Yes, thanks to you." He gave her a long look. "You look tired. Even when Max's sick, he can run the average adult ragged. How on earth do you know what to say to him, what to do with him? Where did you get that magic touch of yours?" He reached for her hand and pressed her palm to his lips.

His mouth was warm, so warm his lips seared her palm. She took a step backward until she hit the refrigerator. His gaze held hers for a long, breathless moment. She had begun to think those sizzling kisses they'd shared had been a fantasy. Until now. Until something flared in his eyes, something she'd never seen before. She'd expected gratitude. It wasn't gratitude. She didn't want gratitude. She didn't know what she wanted until it happened. Until he took her hands and pinned her against the gleaming white refrigerator.

She was trapped. With the smell of coffee in the air and the sunlight streaming through the kitchen window, she saw the desire in his dazzling blue gaze. White-hot desire that matched her own. He bent his head, but before he kissed her he said, "He's right, you are beautiful." His voice dropped to a whisper. "So beautiful."

His words made her melt inside. She was ready for passion, but not for tenderness. He gave her both. Hard, fierce, wild kisses that left her breathless and dying for more. Soft, wet, deep kisses that touched her all the way to her soul. She returned them, kiss for kiss. Wanting to show him that he had too much to give to live his life alone. That it wasn't wrong to love again, to live again. But she knew what he'd say. It *was* wrong to love again. He wasn't going to love again. This wasn't love.

Damn it, he could have fooled her. It felt like love, it looked like love and that was the problem. She was falling in love all over again. All by herself. She should know better, too. Kate's words came rushing back. *You're in a vulnerable state. You'll fall for the first guy who smiles at you.* She'd fallen for Josh Gentry before he'd ever smiled at her. Way before. And if she didn't back off, she'd be rushing headlong for disaster, once again. Giving her heart away to somebody who didn't want it. Who didn't know what to do with it.

She broke the kiss and came up to take a breath of air— a breath of air and a dose of reality. Josh gave her a dazed, quizzical look. The truth was she needed a lot more than air or reality. She needed a stern reminder of her goals in life.

She mumbled something incoherent and untangled herself from his arms. Somehow she found the back door, walked out and across the field without hearing the birds, without seeing the wild poppies waving in the breeze. She got all the way to the barn when she turned around and went back. More than needing a reminder of her goals, she needed to explain them to Josh. He was standing in the doorway watching her walk toward him.

"I'd like to…I need to tell you something," she said, brushing past him on her way into the kitchen.

He motioned her to a chair and sat down across from her.

"I was an only child, see," she said. The words tumbled out so fast she couldn't stop them. "You can't know what it's like, but believe me, it's lonely. So I thought, when I grow up I'm going to have a big family. And a career. Why not? Why not have it all? I got into advertising right after college. It was exciting, fun and challenging. I'm very competitive, and I was good at it. I ended up at one of the biggest agencies, and I fell in love with the boss's son. But not because he was the boss's son. Because he wanted the same things I wanted. Success. Marriage. Kids. It was like a dream come true."

"You felt like a princess," he said.

She gave him a wry smile. "Yes. But I wasn't. It all fell apart. After years of planning how I'd juggle a career with a family, and looking for a man who wanted the same things, to share it all with me, everything went wrong. We lost an account. He thought it was my fault. Maybe it was. Maybe it was his. In any case, he blamed me for it to save his hide. I got fired. He got promoted."

Josh got up and filled her cup with fresh coffee. "Because his father was the boss?"

"That didn't hurt his chances. But actually he's very good at what he does. That's why I've got to succeed at this Wild Mustang account."

"To prove to him that you're as good as he is?"

She took a sip of coffee. "To prove to myself. Though I can't deny I have a desire to show him I can do it. He told me I was too tough and too competitive to be a wife and mother, but I wasn't good enough and didn't have the talent to succeed in advertising." Just repeating the words that once hurt so badly took some of the sting out of them.

"Did you believe him?"

"Not about advertising. I understand the business. I really do. I know I can do it. I *am* doing it. I have my own business, and now this Wild Mustang account. About being a wife and mother... Well, you can't have everything. I know that now. I've decided to concentrate on one thing at a time. That one thing is advertising."

She took a deep breath. "What I want to say is, you don't have to worry about me. About my trying to worm my way into your life or be some kind of substitute mom to Max or anything, as much as I like...love him. Because after the film crew comes and goes, I'm out of here. Back to my real life. I've got plans, big plans. This Wild Mustang thing is just the beginning." She smiled then, a little forced, but it was the best she could do.

"That was quite a speech," he said.

One corner of her mouth tilted up. It wasn't much of a smile, but it was for real.

"Time for lunch," he said. "What'll it be, Campbell's cream of chicken or Campbell's chicken noodle?"

"Whatever you're having."

Over soup and crackers they talked some more about her life. He asked questions about her past and her plans for the future and about what she did every day when she was at home. She hadn't talked so much since she'd given a speech on career day at her old high school. Nobody had ever listened with such rapt attention as he did. Certainly not the high school kids.

"I've talked your ear off," she said, breaking a cracker in two. "You're a good listener."

He reached for her hand for the second time that day and covered it with his. "You're a good talker," he said.

At that moment Max called from his room down the hall. He was hot, hungry and thirsty. Josh told Bridget he'd take care of him, that she should go outside and get some air. She protested, but he shoved her out the door. This time she smelled the roses that climbed the trellis, picked some poppies, felt the sun on her skin, listened to the birds and headed for the corral to look at the wild mustang and note her progress.

She leaned against the fence and watched the mare kick up her heels and whinny. "Hello, girl," she called. "Remember me? I haven't seen you for a while. Not since the day…" Oh, lord, the day Josh told her how much she bothered him, then proceeded to show her just how much. The day she'd lost her head and thrown herself at him. The day he'd cut her off by telling her about Molly and how he'd never love again. The day his mother appeared on the scene and asked her to the birthday party. Yes, that was the day all right. The day she realized this, whatever it was she felt for Josh, was a hopeless cause.

"How do you like it here?" she asked the horse.

The horse galloped up to the fence and stopped abruptly and tossed her head.

"Yes," Bridget said, "that's how I feel too. You're lucky, you know, to belong here. I don't. I wish I did." She lowered her voice to a conspiratorial whisper. "I wish I were part of the family. I love them, you know. I love them both," she said. Then she looked around, feeling foolish confiding in a horse. She told herself to stop this fruitless wishing for what she couldn't have. She would belong to someone someday. If that's really what she wanted. It wouldn't be Max and Josh, but it would be someone who was unattached. It might take a few more years, though. To find the right person. She might very well be in the rest home by then, the way things were going—if she didn't quit falling for the wrong men.

By the time she got back to the house, she felt better able to handle the situation. Josh had fed Max, who was asking for her. She read him a story, then went to mix up some Jell-O she found in the walk-in pantry. Josh asked if she'd mind if he left for an hour to go to his father's place and feed the animals. She offered to make dinner. He looked surprised that she knew how to cook. But he opened the lid to the large freezer saying there ought to be something in there. There was. There was meat and frozen vegetables.

And so went the day. Taking turns with Max, helping out here and there, running a load of laundry, making a stew that simmered on the back burner all afternoon. Making play dough for Max, putting food coloring into it to turn it green. Whipping up a batch of biscuits. If only Kate could see her now, playing Betty Crocker, what would she say?

Bridget, she'd say, *what* are *you doing?*

Doing? I'm helping. Can't you see that?

Helping who? Not yourself. You're digging a hole for yourself. You want them to think you're indispensable. But obody's indispensable.

But they want me, they need me, Bridget protested. *At least for now.*

What about your *wants and* your *needs, Bridgie?*

I know, I know. I just want to be wanted.

Leave. Leave now, before it's too late. Before they break your heart. Both of them.

I can't.

At dusk Max was in the den on the couch watching television. Josh burst into the kitchen, tossed his hat toward the rack at the back door and broke into her reverie. "What were you saying?" he asked.

"Me?" she asked, wiping her hands on her apron. "Nothing."

"Smells great."

She gave the savory mixture a stir. "I was hoping Max might feel like eating, but he says he's not hungry."

Josh went to check on him. He'd dozed off so Josh turned off the TV and put another blanket over him. He laid the back of his hand against his forehead and decided his fever had receded. Josh knew the boy was uncomfortable by the way he scratched his arms even as he slept, but he was no longer so worried about the outcome.

Back in the kitchen where a delicious homey smell filled the air, a feeling of relief and well-being came over him as he shared the latest medical bulletin with Bridget. He hadn't realized how much he'd missed having an adult conversation at the end of the day. Or at lunch. Or in the morning.

Yes, Max was getting better, and Bridget was in his kitchen. He had an overwhelming desire to go to the stove and put his arms around her waist, pull her back until they meshed together. Until her fanny was pressed intimately against his manhood. He would put his hands around her rib cage, and reach under her shirt to rub his knuckles across the soft skin of her abdomen.

He would brush the fullness of her breasts with his thumbs, and she'd turn in his arms, breathless, eager, as responsive as he knew she could be. He'd never known a woman's desire could flare up like that. He wondered, no, he *knew* how passionate she'd be in bed. How generous. His heart started beating like a tractor engine. Loud and strong.

The image of them making love flashed in front of his eyes. He tried to block it, but he could see Bridget in a silk nightgown, her tawny hair falling over her shoulders, brushing against his chest, her breasts freed from that lace bra she wore, teasing and tantalizing him. He took a deep breath. It wasn't going to happen. Because it was wrong. But for the first time he asked himself why.

He gripped the back of the chair to prevent himself from going to the stove and living out his fantasy. It wasn't fair to Bridget to lead her on. He'd made it clear how he felt, and he wouldn't confuse her by giving in to his lust. But that wasn't all it was. He cared about Bridget. The more he learned about her, the more he saw of her, the more he liked her. He liked her *and* he lusted after her. It was a dangerous combination. But it wasn't love. It couldn't be.

She pulled a pan of biscuits out of the oven. Her face was flushed from the heat.

"Biscuits?" he said. "You made biscuits? Where did you learn to cook?" He felt his resolve to keep his hands off her fading. He was strong, but he wasn't made of stone.

"I just learned by trial and error. I like having people over, you know, invite a bunch of friends for dinner, everybody pitches in. I've never made biscuits, though. I found the recipe in that book there." She pointed to Molly's well-worn cookbooks on the shelf. Neither of them mentioned her name. Neither wanted to spoil the mood, to bring someone else onto the scene. But they both knew whose book it was.

Bridget ladled stew into bowls and piled biscuits onto a plate. They sat down at the table and talked and laughed and exchanged lingering looks that only hinted at what they felt. Feelings bubbled to the surface no matter how determined they were to keep them buried deep down where they belonged.

And then the phone rang, the harsh sound interrupting the seamless flow of their conversation. It was Molly's parents. He wanted to tell them everything was okay. He *did* tell them everything was okay, but he had to tell them Max had chicken pox. They were alarmed. They were worried. They said they'd be there tomorrow to help Josh take care of him.

He protested that everything was under control. They insisted. They'd be on the next plane from Scottsdale, rent a car at the airport and make sure their grandson was all right. He hung up and went back to the table. But he couldn't finish his dinner. Reality had intruded on his fantasy—the fantasy that Bridget belonged here.

"That was..." he began.

"I know," she said.

"I couldn't stop them from coming."

"Of course not."

"I told them he was all right, but they're concerned. He's their only grandson."

"I understand," she said. "You won't need me anymore."

"They sold their land and moved to Arizona when Molly graduated from high school," he explained. "But they come back from time to time to see their friends, and Max of course."

"Of course."

He watched her get up and go to the stove to cover the pot. He wanted to blurt out that he needed her more than ever. But he forced himself to say something else.

"Bridget," he said hoarsely, "how can I thank you for what you've done? You've been a lifesaver, a godsend. Don't go back to town tonight. Stay here. Max will miss you if you're not here in the morning." *I'll miss you if you're not here in the morning,* a voice inside him said. *Don't go. You can't go.*

She turned to look at him. She hesitated as if she'd heard his unspoken plea.

"I'll miss him too."

What about me, will you miss me too?

"Tell Max I'll see him...." She grabbed her purse from the counter and was out the door before she could say when or where.

He followed her out the door in the dark to her car. "I don't want you to go like this," he said, raking a hand through his hair in frustration. "I haven't even thanked you for what you've done."

"Yes, you have," she said, speaking to him through the window of her car. "Besides, I enjoyed it. I had a good time. Really." She managed a small smile, but he could have sworn there were tears in her eyes.

She started the motor.

"Wait a minute," he said, but she didn't wait. She pulled away in a shower of gravel, leaving him standing there alone. His chest ached as if there was a weight pressing on his lungs. He couldn't breathe, he couldn't move. He could only stand there staring after her. He didn't know when he'd felt so alone and so lonely.

Yes, he did.

It was when Molly died. Was he destined to go through life losing the people he loved? But he didn't love Bridget, did he? And he hadn't lost her, because you can't lose someone you don't have.

Molly's parents doted on Max. Catered to his every whim. Prepared his favorite foods, brought out a new toy every day and read his favorite stories tirelessly. They cleaned the house from top to bottom, cooked for Josh, and in general took over. Josh was free to get his own work done as well as the work on his parents' ranch. He attacked dirty jobs with a vengeance, the ones he hadn't had time for like priming the pump and cleaning out the stables. Trying like crazy to block the image of Bridget in his house, at the stove, across the table, in his arms.

When he came home at the end of each day, he felt more like a guest in his house. By the end of the week Max was thoroughly spoiled, and while still covered with an itchy red rash, he was not very sick. His disposition was best described as grumpy. Josh felt the same way, but he didn't know why. He was restless and edgy and thoroughly out of sorts. His horses wouldn't cooperate with him. One threw a shoe and the other threw him—right on his back. He wasn't hurt, he was mad.

When he went back to the house, tired and sore and aching, Max demanded that his father bring Bridget back.

Chapter Seven

"Where is she? Why doesn't she come and see me?" Max demanded, scratching his stomach. "I'm bored," he said tossing a plastic toy soldier across his room. He didn't want to stay in bed, but he got tired so fast he couldn't stay up more than a half hour before he was exhausted. Josh was tearing his hair. Literally raking his hands through it until it stood out in every direction. He understood how Max felt. He too was restless and bored, and he too wanted to see Bridget. But he *didn't* have chicken pox. He had no excuse for feeling this way.

His in-laws had left, and his parents were back in town. They'd been by to take a turn with Max, but they had things to do, and now it was back to just Max and Josh. From now on. Finally Josh gave in and called Bridget. After all, it was only natural to give her an update on Max's condition. After he dialed the number of the woman Bridget rented the room from, and she promised to go knock on her door, Josh handed the phone to Max. Then he leaned back, not even realizing he was holding his breath while he waited. She might be out. She probably was out. For all he knew she'd gone back to San Francisco.

But she hadn't. Not yet. Max was so excited to talk to her, his red blotchy face got even redder. His voice was so loud Josh could have heard him from the kitchen. Straining to hear the other end of the conversation, his fingers itched to grab the phone out of Max's hands. Max was listing the presents he'd received from his grandparents and all the TV shows he'd watched, then he begged her to come and see him.

"I made something out of the play dough you gave me," he said. "I wanna show it to you. When are you coming to see me?"

Josh bent over, trying to hear her answer. He couldn't hear anything. The question echoed in his head. When are you coming to see me? When, when, when. After an eternity Max finally handed the receiver to him.

"She wants to talk to you," Max said.

"Hi," she said.

Just the sound of her voice threw his carefully controlled emotions into turmoil. Just when he thought things were getting back to normal, Max getting well, Molly's parents gone, his parents back, something made him call her. He didn't *have* to call her. He'd wanted to call her. He was using Max as an excuse to call her.

"I've missed you," he blurted. What was wrong with him. Why hadn't he practiced this conversation before he took the phone. "It's seems like a long time." It seemed like forever since he'd seen her smile at him across the table, seen her hazel eyes light up at something he said, felt the warmth of her hand in his. "I'd...we'd both like to see you. If you've got any time, that is. My mother was just here. She left some food."

At that, Max, who was bouncing up and down on his

mattress with excitement, grabbed the phone out of Josh's hand.

"It's fried chicken," he yelled into the phone. "And potato salad. And tapioca pudding. She made it for me. But you can have some, too."

When Josh got the phone back, Bridget was laughing. "Are you sure it's all right," she asked.

"It's more than all right," he said. "It's imperative."

Bridget tied her hair back with a scarf to keep cool, put on a pair of shorts and a T-shirt and went down to her car. The hot dry wind blew tufts of sagebrush across Main Street. A woman stepped out of the bakery and waved to her. Bridget waved back. There had been moments during this past week when she thought of going back to San Francisco—just until Max got well and they could proceed with the photo session.

But the thought of the cool gray city by the bay with hordes of people rushing around and horns honking didn't hold any attraction for her. She knew her friends would think she was crazy, spending her free time walking in the hills above the town, taking pictures of a occasional wildflower under a cloudless sky and finding beauty in the stark landscape.

It was strange how her life back there seemed so far away. And so insignificant, she thought. She had no desire to reenter the rat race. There was really nothing she could do until Max got well. So she'd just stay there in Harmony, and try not to think about the most intriguing, most rugged, most down-to-earth, honest man she'd ever met. Too honest. He'd made it clear he'd never fall in love again. Never get married again. In short, he was unavailable. And yet, as soon as he called her, she was running to see him, making herself available anytime he called, anytime he said he missed her. This was the last time, positively the last.

She argued with herself all the way to the ranch. Told

herself she was going to see Max. That he was sick and he needed her. That was partly true. She'd missed the little boy. She'd worried about him, pictured his pock-marked face, his glazed eyes, his feverish brow and wondered how he was doing. He sounded full of energy this morning. So much energy it took more than one adult to cope with him.

She shook her head, wondering how—if he were hers, and she was a single parent—she could possibly handle him. Since the first day she'd seen him, a tangle of cuts and bruises and dirty legs, and he'd put his hand into hers to lead her up the hill to his house, she'd felt a kinship with him. And even more, she'd felt responsible for him, even though he'd run into her.

And then she'd met his father. Was it her imagination or had he changed since that fateful day she'd stood outside the fence taking pictures? Well, he'd changed his mind about being the representative of Wild Mustang men's cologne. Other than that, he was just as gruff, just as determined, just as stubborn as he'd ever been.

There were other qualities she hadn't noticed that day. There was passion, there was tenderness and there was loyalty. The passion and the tenderness he was willing to give. And she was more than willing to take. But the loyalty was unswerving. And it was reserved for another woman. A dead woman. This was important to remember, because when she saw him, she was likely to forget. She was likely to concentrate on what she could have and not what she couldn't have. On what he could give and not on what he couldn't.

When she arrived back at the ranch, she slipped back into their lives as if she'd never been gone, as if she was part of their lives, when in reality she'd only spent that one day there. She molded play dough figures with Josh, ate fried chicken with them at lunchtime, and forgot about what she was supposed to remember, until Max took a nap and she had coffee with Josh at the kitchen table.

"Did your parents enjoy their vacation?" Bridget asked, keeping the conversation light, away from the personal. Away from anything that mattered.

"Yes, but they felt terrible when they heard Max was sick."

"How was the weather in San Francisco?" she asked.

"Foggy."

"Figures. You know I haven't worn shorts in the summer for years. Since I went to Girl Scout camp. I think I'm getting freckles. At my advanced age."

He tilted his chair back and let his eyes roam over her body. She felt the heat from his gaze as it lingered here and there. "On you they look good."

"What?" It was an effort to keep her voice steady when he unnerved her so with just a look. She couldn't even pick up her coffee cup for fear of spilling it all over the table. "The shorts or the freckles?"

"Both," he said with a sexy grin.

If she didn't know better, if she didn't know he was the most unavailable unmarried man she'd ever met, she would have sworn he was flirting with her.

"Did something happen this week?" she asked, a tiny flicker of hope stirring in her breast. Maybe he'd changed his mind about devoting his life to the memory of a dead woman.

"Did something happen?" he asked. "My son got sick, my in-laws were here, my parents went away and came back. You were here. And now you're back. That's the best part. Why do you ask?"

She studied his face. "Just wondering. You seem different."

"I'm relieved. Max is getting well. The worst is over." He stood and pulled her out of her chair. Despite her resolve, her fingers closed around his wrists. "I missed you so much," he said, his voice husky with emotion.

Goose bumps rose all over her arms and bare legs. Drums beat a rhythm in her ears, almost drowning out the warnings. She ached to feel his arms around her, to feel his mouth come down on hers, hard and demanding. She longed to slip her hands inside his denim shirt, press her palms against the muscles of his chest and feel his heart beat in time to hers. But this was not going to happen. She was a fool if she thought she had a chance at happiness with him, with someone who had loved once and would never love again.

He ran his hands down her arms, settled on her waist. She stiffened. He sensed her hesitation and drew back to look at her, furrowed lines deepening across his forehead. She broke away, went to the sink, took a drink of water, then turned to face him.

"This was a mistake," she said. "I shouldn't have come. I can't come here anymore, Josh."

"I've asked too much of you, haven't I?" he asked, frowning. "Taking care of Max. I'm sorry."

"No, that's not it. It's just the opposite. You haven't asked enough."

"I thought you liked it here," he said. "You fit in so well."

"I do like it, I like it too much. But I don't fit in. There's no room for me here. If I don't break away now, I...I—" Her voice broke. She swallowed hard. "It's my own fault. When I came here to Harmony I was in a vulnerable state. Feeling good about my career, but terrible about my personal life. I told you how I'd been dumped and it would be only natural the next man who came along—"

"The next man," he said, "meaning me."

"Yes, you. You're so solid, so honest. I couldn't help but see the contrast. I lost my head a little bit. I really like you, Josh.'' She bit her lip. "But from now on it's got to be strictly business between us and that's all. Not that it was ever really more," she assured him. "But I can't keep hanging around here, trying to fit in, when I really don't fit in at all."

"Max told my in-laws about you," he said, straddling the kitchen chair. "And they told me they'd understand if I found someone I wanted to marry. I think they would almost welcome it in a way."

"Maybe to give Max a mother," she suggested soberly.

"I wouldn't do that. I'd never marry someone just so Max could have a mother. It wouldn't be fair to her. The fact is that everyone—my parents, as well as my in-laws—wants me to remarry. They don't seem to understand." The frustration in his voice was unmistakable.

Bridget wanted to blurt out that she understood, as well as anyone could who hadn't lost a loved one. For all she knew she'd do just the same. Swear off love forever.

"I shouldn't expect them to understand how I feel. No one can unless they've gone through it."

"But, Josh…" She hesitated only a moment, then she took a deep breath and continued, because if she didn't say it now, she'd never say it. "Okay, you're the only one who knows how you feel. You're the only one who's gone through it. But maybe people like your parents think you've spent enough time mourning. Don't you agree that life is too short to cut yourself off from love? When you have so much to give. Not that you, not that I—"

He shook his head. He didn't want to hear another word. Not from her. Not from anyone. He was tired of being told what he should do and how he should feel. No one knew how he really felt. How he struggled with guilt every time he thought about Molly, wishing he'd been a better husband, a better person. He could never compound that guilt by falling in love with someone else, someone so different, so completely different. Someone who didn't belong here, who'd leave the minute she realized what life was really like in Harmony. "'Not that you know anything about it,' is that what you were going to say?" he asked.

"I know that I wouldn't wish a lonely life on anyone," she said, crossing her arms at her waist.

"What makes you think my life is lonely?" he said, knocking his chair over with a loud bang in his haste to get to his feet. "I have a son, parents, sisters. You're the one with the lonely life. Is that why you're telling me this? Because you're projecting your own feelings on me? Because if you are, I don't want to hear it. Save your advice for someone who wants it." He didn't mean for his words to sound so harsh and so unfeeling. But that's the way they came out.

Bridget winced as if he'd struck her, then shivered as if she felt the chill in the air. She opened her mouth to say something, but she must have changed her mind. Without speaking, she turned and marched out the door, her chin in the air. He watched her go, already regretting the way he'd lashed out at her. Wishing he could stop her. Wishing he could take his words back. Because although part of what he said was true, he'd lied to her. He *was* lonely. Lonelier now since he'd met her than he'd ever been.

She was right about one thing. He'd certainly heard it all before. Could everyone but him be wrong? Right or wrong, hearing it again from an outsider, realizing that even a stranger could size up his situation in such a short time and be so damned outspoken had just made him mad. Mad and even more determined to never love again. To never hurt again. It didn't matter what anyone thought. No one knew how he felt but himself.

Granted, it was a lonely life, but it was his life. He was so tired of hearing people tell him how he should live it. It was bad enough hearing it from his parents, then his parents-in-law. But to hear it from Bridget, too, had pushed him over the edge. Still it didn't give him the right to hurt her like that. He sighed and went to check on Max.

When Bridget called him the next day, she kept her voice as frosty as a morning in winter and asked him when to schedule the photographers. She was holding her appointment calendar in her hands, so afraid he'd tell her to forget the whole thing her hands shook. But he didn't. He said one more week ought to do it. Max would be completely over the chicken pox. She wrote down the times and dates in a shaky scrawl she could barely read. Gathering her courage, she asked if he knew where the three-man crew could stay overnight. He volunteered the spare room in his house as long as it was only for a night.

She was surprised—no, she was outright shocked at this display of magnanimousness. She thought for sure he'd tell them to sleep in tents in the pasture. Or at a hotel in Reno, three hours away. She assured him they'd bring sandwiches from the diner for their lunch and go back to town for dinner. He thanked her, she thanked him. Magnanimous or not, his voice was as cool as hers. He was all business, just as she wanted it—the way it had to be.

If that was the way she wanted it, why did she feel like going back to bed and pulling the covers over her head?

She should be glad. After a two-week delay, everything was moving like clockwork. She had the two-day shoot completely planned out on paper, down to the last detail—closeups with horse and without; in the corral and out; on the hill; in the pasture. She was pleased, but she wasn't happy. How could she be, when she knew that Josh saw her as a pathetic, lonely creature, clinging to him and his son for companionship? No, he hadn't said it in so many words. He didn't have to. She got the message.

She didn't go back to bed and pull the covers over her

head. Recalling Kate's motto, "When the going gets tough, the tough go shopping," she went down to the dry goods store and bought souvenirs for her friends at home. It was a way of saying to herself, I *am* going home. I have a home and I'm going there. I have friends, too. She was trying to drown out the words, the words that haunted her ever since he'd spoken them. *You're the one with the lonely life.*

She bought a pair of silver earrings and a slew of bright cotton scarves. After trying on a dozen hats, she settled on a soft white buckskin resistol for Kate, and for her father, a hand-tooled leather belt with silver studs like the one she bought for Josh's father. Feeling a little bit better with every purchase, she bought herself a new pair of white Wrangler jeans and a white Western-style shirt fringed with red and a red scarf to wear to Suzy's party. Then she broke down and bought herself a hat and boots.

When she came out of the tiny dressing room to look in the mirror, the owner smiled her approval. "You look like Miss Rodeo," she said.

"That's what I'm afraid of. I've overdone it, haven't I?" she said, frowning at herself in the mirror. There she went again. Trying to be something she wasn't. Trying to fit in and botching it. She wasn't Miss Rodeo. She was Miss City Girl. She shook her head at the image in the full-length mirror. She loved the outfit, she really did. But did she have the nerve to wear it? Before she could change her mind, she changed back into her clothes, put the outfit on the counter and told the woman she'd take it. All of it. Everything.

On the day of the party she compromised by wearing her own white linen shorts, the new shirt, scarf and handcrafted silver earrings. Leaving the boots and hat and jeans back in the room, she walked down Main Street toward Suzy's house, the little house with the big yard on Sandstone Street. Bridget would have been nervous if she thought Josh would be there. But she felt sure he wouldn't. Not after that speech he'd given her.

Josh would certainly have no more wish to run into her than she would to run into him. It was bad enough they had to work together when the photographers came. He wouldn't be looking forward to it any more than she was. He must be regretting the day he decided to be her Wild Mustang Man. It was to his credit that he hadn't backed out. A lesser man would have.

As for herself, Bridget planned to grit her teeth and get through two days of shooting somehow, then pack her bags and go home. But if she thought he'd be there today, she never would have left her room above the shoe repair shop.

When Bridget arrived, Suzy's big grassy yard, which wrapped around her small house, was already full of people, music and smoke from the barbecue. Suzy rushed to the gate to meet her.

"You look terrific," Suzy said, stepping back to get the full effect of Bridget's outfit. Bridget blushed at the compliment but was reassured. Suzy was so warm, so sincere, she made her feel welcome and appropriately dressed for a Western barbecue. Bridget liked her more every time she saw her. "All you need is a hat and boots," Suzy added.

Bridget bit her lip to keep from blurting that she *had* the hat and boots and someday, somewhere, she'd wear them.

"Come and meet the gang," Suzy said taking her by the hand to make introductions.

Within a few minutes Bridget was in the middle of a group of friendly men Suzy described as the "movers and shakers" of their high school class. She was busy answering their questions about the advertising business, when out of the corner of her eye she saw Josh. She stammered and stumbled over her words before she pulled herself together. It was too late to leave, but there were enough people there that she might be able to avoid him all afternoon. It was worth a try.

She shifted the conversation to "the movers and shakers" and let them talk about themselves, and all the while she felt Josh's gaze on her. She could almost feel his hostility radiating across the wide grassy yard. He hadn't forgiven her for butting into his life and telling him how to live it. That made them even. Because she hadn't forgiven him for the misplaced pity he felt for her.

Apparently she didn't try hard enough to avoid him because just as she lined up for the buffet spread out on two long tables, he came up behind her. She held her breath. She wasn't going to speak to him unless he spoke first. And he didn't look like he was going to speak at all. Then why was he standing behind her, breathing down her neck? Yes, she could feel his warm breath against her hair, making her spine tingle. The noise and laughter swirled around them, but all she could think of was Josh. If he didn't say something soon she'd do something desperate like...like—

"Having a good time?" he said at last.

She took a plate and heaped a large helping of green salad on it. "Yes, thank you," she said without a glance in his direction.

"Don't thank me," he said.

"I'm not. It's just a figure of speech." She spooned some baked beans onto her plate so vigorously they splashed on her new shirt. "Oh, damn," she muttered.

"Here, let me." Before she could jerk away, he'd pulled out his handkerchief and was mopping up the brown juice just under the red fringe of her shirt. Just under the fringe and just over her breast. Despite her efforts to be cool and detached, his touch caused her nipples to harden and peak under the soft cotton. By the gleam in his eyes and the smile he was trying to smother, he knew what he'd done and he wasn't one bit sorry. Damn him.

If he didn't know it now, he would soon know how upset she was. Just as she was about to let loose with an angry outburst, in a refined and dignified way, of course, Josh casually fingered the fringe on her shirt.

"Nice shirt," he said. "All you need is a hat and boots."

"All I need is a glass of cold water to throw in your face." A sheepskin jacket would be nice, too, to conceal her traitorous body's response to his touch. But she would have to get along without either the water or the jacket. She'd just have to get herself under control. She'd have to forget how it felt to have him cup her breasts in his hands, brush her nipples with his thumbs. Her face flamed at the memory. He misread the high color in her cheeks.

"You're mad. I understand that. I was way out of line, talking to you the way I did the other day. After all you've done for me."

"Forget all I've done for you," she said hotly. "I don't want your gratitude."

"What do you want, Bridget?" he asked softly.

Your heart. That's what I want. But it isn't yours to give. Not anymore. The words she could never say stuck in her throat "Nothing," she said. "I have everything I want, thanks to your agreeing to be the Wild Mustang Man. I'm the one who's grateful to you. Not to mention the fact that you're having the crew overnight. I appreciate that."

He shrugged. "Where else could they stay? Besides, Max is looking forward to them coming. He wants to take pictures, too. Ever since that day you let him use your camera, he's been talking about it. Making movies, being in the movies. Maybe he'll turn out to be a cinematographer."

"I thought you'd want him to tame wild mustangs like you do."

"He couldn't care less about horses. I've given up on that."

"So you wouldn't mind if he turned the barn into a sound studio?"

"As long as it doesn't scare my horses."

A tall man in a wide-brimmed hat came up behind Josh and slapped him on the back. "Gentry," he said. "I'll be damned if it isn't our class president. God, it's good to see you. Sorry to hear about Molly."

Bridget froze. Watching, waiting to hear what he'd say.

"Thanks," Josh said. "How've you been, Dave?"

She exhaled. That was it. If only he felt the way he sounded, resigned but ready to move on. But she knew he didn't.

"Good. Hey, your son gonna be a football player like you?"

Josh shook his head. "Not interested in football. Or horses. Only thing he cares about is riding his bike. Wants a motorbike next. And he's only five."

"Give him time. He'll come around," Dave said, spearing a piece of barbecued chicken. "What about a little scrimmage after lunch in the backyard. You up for that?"

"I don't know. Haven't played since that last game senior year."

"Homecoming," Dave said with a nostalgic smile. "We beat Anniston thirteen to twenty-one. What a game. I kept the football. And I brought the picture from the front page of the *Harmony Times*. Heard you'd be here today." He reached into his shirt pocket for a yellowed clipping. "Here's you, here's me," he said proudly.

Bridget leaned over his shoulder. The face that looked up out of the old clipping was the all-American boy, so young, so tough, with the mud-splattered football uniform, and yet so vulnerable her heart stopped. What if she'd known him then? He wouldn't have looked twice at her,

Bridget told herself. He was in love with his Molly. Bridget dragged her gaze from the old newspaper. Tally spotted her and waved her over to her table. A few minutes later, Josh had found a place at the table between her and Tally's husband, Jed. Bridget turned and gave him her coolest look, the one that said, if you want to avoid me, if you find me such a buttinski, an annoying thorn in your side, then why are you following me around this party?

By the way he'd wedged himself onto the bench next to her, he seemed oblivious to her apparent dislike for him, and he seemed determined to throw himself into the conversation with his old friends and classmates, to show everyone he hadn't become a hermit or a recluse.

"I'll never forget that night after the prom at the beach," Jed said. "By shoving me in your car when I was drunk, you probably saved my life, Josh. I don't think I ever thanked you for that."

"No need," Josh said. "You would have done the same for me."

"I guess none of us has forgotten that night," Tally said softly. "And the wishes we made."

Bridget held her breath. They talked as if she'd been there, and she almost felt like she had, hearing them all wish on a star as they sat on the sandy beach. Tally turned to Bridget, as if she suddenly remembered that she hadn't been there.

"What would you have wished for, Bridget?" she asked. "If you'd been there."

"Me? I...I don't know," she said, conscious of Josh's thigh pressed next to hers, his arm brushing hers as he set his glass of beer on the table. "I guess I've always wanted to find love and happiness, and I also wanted to accomplish something. I'm not quite there yet," she said wistfully.

"You're getting close, though, aren't you?" Tally asked.

"With Josh as your Wild Mustang Man you'll surely accomplish something. You'll make him famous."

He shook his head. "I never wished for fame," he said soberly. "All I ever wanted…"

"I know," Tally said. "I remember. To live the same kind of life your parents lived. To have what they had. It seemed like you had it all within your grasp. I remember thinking that night that you had everything. I was so envious I could hardly stand to be around you. I was feeling pretty sorry for myself."

"As I remember, sweetheart, you didn't sound one bit sorry for yourself," her husband said. "You had your career all planned out, how you were going to work hard and get a horse of your own, then a ranch."

"That was just talk. An act I put on so no one would feel sorry for me. I never really thought I'd have those things. But I couldn't let on. Nobody wants pity."

Bridget glanced at Josh. He was looking at her. For just a moment their glances held. And in that moment she knew that he realized how badly he'd hurt her by what he'd said. How badly she'd hated being on the receiving end of his pity.

Tally broke the serious mood by going to get coffee for everyone. The talk went back to happier times, to memories of class pranks and dances and sports. Bridget listened, amazed at how different Josh seemed from the angry man she'd first met in his bathroom. Relaxed, easy-going, recalling old teachers, telling stories, laughing and joking. Was this all an act to show her and everyone else he was fine, to prove to her especially that he wasn't lonely, that he not only had a big family, he had friends, as well? If it was an act, it was a good one.

After lunch people drifted away to play touch football on the side lawn. Somebody called Josh to join them, but he lingered at the table. Bridget lingered, too, though she knew she should get up and mingle. But with the sun filtering through the cottonwood tree that shaded Suzy's house, a cup of coffee in front of her, warmed by the companionship as well as the sun, she just didn't want to move.

But when she saw she and Josh were the only ones left, she pressed her palms against the table and looked around nervously.

"Don't go," he said, capturing her wrists in his callused hands. "I want to talk to you."

"I thought you'd said it all the other day," she said, looking down at his large hands, hands that could tame a wild horse, soothe a sick child or drive a woman crazy with desire.

"I said too much," he said. "About your having a lonely life. I didn't know what I was talking about. You don't have a lonely life. You couldn't have. You attract people like…"

"Like flies, is that what you were going to say?" she asked.

He let her hands go and brushed her cheek with his knuckles, a sensual gesture that caused her to tremble. "Like honey. Like bees to honey. That guy that let you go. He was a fool. An idiot. You're better off without him. But you know that. What you don't know is that you'll find someone else. Hell, you don't even have to look. He'll find you. You'll have success, too, and you'll have someone who will love you for what you are—a…a…" Josh wanted to say a gorgeous woman, a beautiful woman, inside and out, but he didn't. If he did, he'd embarrass both her and himself.

He was trying to make up for the other day when he'd hurt her feelings, but he couldn't seem to say what he felt— that she was warm, sweet, sexy and beautiful. It was true, but he couldn't say it. It was also true that she'd made him feel alive again, that he wanted her more than he'd ever

wanted anything. Including Molly. Molly was his boyhood
dream. Bridget was his adult fantasy. He couldn't say that,
either. He shouldn't even think it. Because the way she was
sitting there, her beautiful hazel eyes flecked with green
gazing at him expectantly, he had a strange feeling that she
could read his mind.

"Yes?" she asked, a smile tilting the corners of her
mouth. "Go on." Her mouth tempted him. He knew exactly how it would feel if he kissed her now. So soft, so
warm, so responsive. Her anger had melted as fast as the
springtime thaw. If he was lucky, she'd kiss him back. A
whole string of hot, passionate kisses that would cause his
heart to shift into overdrive.

He leaned forward—and caught himself just in time.
What was he thinking? He couldn't do it, couldn't kiss her
now, not even once. Because once wasn't enough. Once
led to twice, and then he'd lose count, right in the middle
of this picnic with everyone he'd ever known within shout-
ing distance. What would they think? They'd think he was
the luckiest son of a gun in the world, he realized, to have
found someone like Bridget. And to have found love twice
in his life. Love? Who said anything about love? What he
felt for her was something else. It had to be. He just didn't
know what to call it.

Chapter Eight

Tired of waiting for the football star to join the game, Suzy organized three-legged sack races. When they were over, two of Josh's former teammates came to get him, dragged him away from the table and tossed him the football. He caught it just as easily as he'd done fifteen years ago and ran down the length of Suzy's backyard for a touchdown As he jogged back to the huddle he saw that Bridget was still at the table, engaged in animated conversation with some women from his class. It was almost as if she belonged there.

Bridget had a way of fitting in, he noticed, whether it was with his family or his classmates. It startled him to see her in that Western outfit, elbows on the table, chattering away as if she was a native Harmonian. But there was more to Bridget than that. There was her guts, as Suzy put it, there was her caring, nurturing side—witness her care of Max when he was sick—and there was her playfulness, as he'd seen in the video she'd made with Max. And that wasn't all....

To his surprise the women jumped up from the table and joined the game, spreading themselves out among the two teams as if they'd planned it. Bridget became a foreword linebacker on the other team, and before the kickoff she stared across the chalk line at him, her hands on her knees.

"You haven't got a chance, you know that, don't you?" he asked.

"Why not? You haven't played for years, I understand," Bridget said.

"No, but when we did, we beat every team in our conference."

"That was then, this is now. If you ask me, you shouldn't rest on your laurels. You looked a little rusty out there," Bridget teased.

"I looked rusty? We'll see who looks rusty," he said with a menacing glare.

"Besides, this is touch football, isn't it? And I come from a long line of fast runners. Have I told you how my father ran the San Francisco Marathon when he was eighty?"

"Talk about resting on your laurels. I'd advise you to rest on your own laurels, if you have any, rather than on your father's. When was the last time you ran the marathon, by the way?"

"Well…"

"No further questions," he said, reaching across the line of scrimmage to tousle her hair.

Josh was so wrapped up watching the fringe on her shirt sway back and forth, giving him tantalizing glimpses of her lace bra and enjoying bantering with her, he forgot about the game. Good thing this wasn't a conference game. He could see the headlines now in the *Harmony Times*. "Quarterback blows it. Can't keep mind on game. More interested in scoring *with* opposition than against it."

Before he knew it, someone had handed the ball to

Bridget and shoved her across the line of scrimmage toward the goal. She zigged around Josh, she zagged around his buddy Dave and took off like a deer, her teammates screaming encouragement. He had to admit, she did run fast, but not as fast as he did. He'd teach her not to brag. He'd almost caught her when a guy named Pete reached her first, tagged her so hard she fell flat on the ground, tripping the woman next to her who tumbled on top of Suzy who was on top of Pete who was on top of Bridget.

Josh couldn't breathe. He wasn't going to breathe again until he got Bridget out from under all those bodies. He hadn't fallen, he hadn't stumbled, but he felt like he'd been tackled by a 240-pound linebacker and had the breath knocked out of him. Frantically he pulled people off the pile. She couldn't be hurt. She had to be all right. It was just a game. While everyone else was laughing and groaning as they staggered to their feet, she was still lying there. His throat ached too much to even speak her name. His heart pounded as he knelt at her side.

"Bridget," he said finally, gently rolling her over on her side. "Are you all right?"

"Oooooh," she said, slowly opening her eyes. "What happened?"

"Is she okay?"

"Should I call a doctor?"

She lifted herself to a sitting position. "No, no, I'm fine."

"Are you sure?" Josh asked, removing blades of grass from her cheek.

"Just had the wind knocked out of me," she said, taking a deep breath. "Did we win?"

Josh exchanged a relieved look with Suzy, who said, "I told you, she's got guts, that girl. Glad she didn't lose them on the field in the line of duty. Time for dessert, everybody," she said, deliberately drawing the attention away from Bridget as Josh lifted her in his arms and carried her to a shady spot under a tree.

"I still don't know what happened," Bridget said, rubbing her head.

"Do you know your name?" he asked.

"This is a test, isn't it, to see if I have a concussion?"

"Well, do you?"

"Am I Knute Rockne?"

"Who's president?"

"Millard Fillmore?"

"That's not funny. I was worried about you," he said. *Worried* wasn't the word. He was scared out of his mind when he saw her lying motionless on the ground. He couldn't take any more accidents or illnesses. Not from those he loved.

There he went again, thinking he loved Bridget, when he couldn't possibly love her. He couldn't, and he wouldn't. It was bad enough he had to worry about Max getting sick or in an accident. He was not going to worry about Bridget, too. But damn it, it was too late. This afternoon he'd almost had a heart attack seeing those bodies pile up on top of her.

"I think I'd like some dessert," she said.

He stood up and looked down at her. "Sure?"

"If it's chocolate, I want some."

"Stay there," he said, and he went to the house to get something chocolate and some coffee with an extra helping of common sense before he lost his head completely. There was little or no common sense to be found in Suzy's little kitchen, where a dozen or so of his old classmates were crowded together laughing and reminiscing about old times.

"There he is, the football hero."

"Josh, the Wild Mustang Man."

"Hey, what does that cologne smell like?"

"What do you think?" Josh asked. "It smells like horses."

This reply brought more laughter, retorts and suggestions for what he could do with it.

"I *like* the name," Tally said. "And I'm going to buy some for Jed as soon as it comes out."

"Save your money," Marshall, the town banker, said. "Jed already smells like a horse."

Jed took a mock swing at Marshall, who ducked and knocked his coffee on the floor.

"Watch it," Josh cautioned. "Bridget might hear you. This is her project. She gets defensive if you knock it."

"I don't blame her," Suzy said, cutting the large chocolate cake into squares. "It's a great idea, and having Josh for the Wild Mustang Man is nothing short of brilliant. Where is she, anyway? Is she okay?"

"Outside," Josh said, gesturing toward the lawn. "I'm taking her a piece of cake."

"I'll take it," Suzy said, grabbing a plate and heading out the back door.

Josh followed her but was waylaid by Jed and Tally. Though the fellow classmates had married only recently, he hadn't gone to their wedding. Hell, he hadn't gone anywhere for the past two years. Now that he was here, among old friends, and it felt so comfortable and natural, he wondered why.

"It's good to see you again, Josh," Tally said, settling on a picnic bench as the late-afternoon shadows fell over Suzy's lawn.

Her husband set his coffee cup next to Jed's and sat down next to him. "Congratulations on your marriage, you two."

The way they looked at each other, eyes brimming with love, filled Josh with painful jealousy. "I have to say I was surprised," Josh said. "I mean, after all these years."

"What do you mean, surprised?" Jed said, reaching for Tally's hand across the table. "You were there that night after the prom. You heard me promise to marry Tally if she wasn't married by our fifteenth reunion."

"Yes, but—"

"But you never thought he'd do it," Tally said. "Neither did I."

"We were crazy kids," Jed said with a smile. "Wishing on a star like that. I must say I was skeptical. But it worked." He caught himself. "Oh, God, Josh, I'm sorry."

"It's all right. I got my wish. I married Molly. The only girl I ever loved."

"But not the only girl you ever *will* love," Tally said softly. "Is she?" Josh's eyes strayed across the yard to where Bridget was sitting with Suzy, and he knew what Tally was thinking. The same thing everyone else was thinking. He clenched his jaw. Not this again. Not someone else telling him to take another chance on love. With Bridget. A woman who didn't belong in Harmony. Who, when she realized how dull life in Harmony was, would be back in San Francisco so fast she'd barely have a chance to say goodbye.

"Those wishes we made that night, those promises... You took them seriously," Josh said to Jed. "You must have, or you wouldn't have come back fifteen years later to make good on them. I feel the same. Finding someone else, loving someone else, especially someone who doesn't belong here, it's not in the cards for me."

"But..." Tally said.

"Leave it," her husband said, putting his hand on her arm. "Josh is doing what he has to do."

"I know," Tally said. "It's just that I can't help thinking how young we were then, how naive. What I'm trying to say is that if I die first, I want you to marry again, Jed. I thought I was happy all those years I was single, but now that I'm married…'' She gave Jed a blissful, intimate smile that made Josh ache inside. "I wouldn't wish the single state on anyone. Not that you should marry just anyone," she added hastily.

Josh didn't know if she was talking to him or her husband. He took a deep breath, hoping to quash this marriage business once and for all. "If you're thinking of Bridget," he said to Tally.

"Who, me?" she asked with mock innocence.

"Bridget is a career girl," Josh explained. "She's very dedicated and focused on making a success in advertising. She has her own company, this is her first big account and for her it's just the beginning of a lucrative career. I'm sure you wouldn't want her to throw it all over for…for a boring life in a small town." The more he said, the more he convinced himself Bridget would be a fool to give up a brilliant career in a sophisticated big city for a humdrum life on a ranch. Taking care of one five-year-old and an overgrown vegetable garden and a house designed by and for someone else? Why would she? She wouldn't. By the time he'd finished his coffee he was thoroughly depressed. Jed and Tally went to help clean up the kitchen, leaving Josh to stare across the yard at Bridget and ponder the situation.

Yet Bridget had seemed happy whenever she was at his ranch. She looked happy, whether she was sitting across the kitchen table from him, eating soup, or making figures out of play dough with Max. But that's because the ranch was a novelty to her. So was he. Once she got back to the city she would realize just how boring life in Harmony was. She'd thank her lucky stars she hadn't made the mistake of staying there. What was wrong with him? He was talking like that was an option. It wasn't.

Dusk was falling. People were leaving. Bridget was standing, saying goodbye to his former classmates. He crossed the yard in a few wide strides. "Are you leaving?" he asked her. "Need a ride?"

"I walked."

"That was before you got tackled."

"I'm fine," she said.

"I insist," he said, taking her by the arm.

They thanked Suzy. They said goodbye to everybody else, then he helped her into the passenger seat of his truck.

"I had a good time," she said as he drove slowly down Main Street toward her room over the shoe repair shop.

"So did I," he said.

"You sound surprised."

"I guess I am." He suddenly remembered why he'd come to the party in the first place. It was to prove to himself that Bridget wasn't the only woman in the world. That she didn't stand out from the crowd like a long-stemmed rose in a petunia patch. So much for that plan. The only thing he'd proven today was that he cared more about Bridget than he'd imagined possible. That he worried about her, thought about her, and didn't want to let her out of his sight. He hated to think what it all added up to.

"So you were president of your class as well as a football star," she said with a sidelong glance at him.

"It's been downhill ever since," he said with a wry smile. "Until now. I feel better than I have in years. I didn't realize it, but I'd missed the old gang. I'd buried myself in my work."

"Since Molly died?" she asked.

"Even before. We got all wound up in our own projects, Molly in her good works, I with the horses. I thought I wanted it that way. Now I see there was something missing. I care about these people."

"They certainly care about you," she said.

"Seems they care about you, too," he said.

"Right," she said. "That's why they tackled me, threw

me to the ground and piled on top of me. I'd hate to see what would have happened if they didn't care about me.''

"I thought you didn't get hurt."

"I didn't. I'm fine. It was more fun than I've had in years.''

"Was it fun to lie on the ground pretending to be unconscious? I didn't need that kind of scare." He pulled up in front of the shuttered shoe repair shop and turned off the engine.

"I'm sorry," she said turning in her seat to face him. "I didn't know touch football could be so rough. Next time I'll stick to the sack races."

"I have to admit you ran pretty fast."

"I told you."

"Other people care about you, too," he said. "Tally and Jed. They just got married this year."

"In their thirties. Maybe there's hope for me," she said, twisting around to look at the clock on the dashboard.

He ran his hand around the steering wheel. Anything to keep from grabbing her by the shoulders and kissing her until he heard her moan with ecstasy, until she returned his kisses, each one hotter and more insistent than the last. Or taking the fringe on her shirt and rubbing it between his fingers, grazing her breasts softly but deliberately until she begged him to go beyond the fringe. Then he'd unbutton her shirt, watching her eyes widen and soften, until he'd tossed it into the back seat.

Next to go would be the white lacy bra he would unhook to let her creamy breasts swell and fill his hands. Oh, Lord, what was wrong with him, letting his imagination run wild like this. The cab of his truck had become unbearably warm, as if he'd left the heater on. He rolled his window down to let the evening air cool his fevered brow and still his pounding pulse. He racked his brain to try to remember what they were talking about. Something about her having hope. Hope of getting married. She couldn't, she wouldn't marry someone else.

"I thought you were into your career these days. That's what I told them," he said desperately.

"Oh, I am. I just thought one of these days...when I feel secure in my work and I find the right person."

Josh felt a stab of jealousy as sharp as a knife in his chest. "How will you find him?" he asked.

"That's the problem. What if I make another mistake? I wonder if I've learned anything. How will I find him? How will I know if I've found him? I'm afraid to trust myself. To know who's right and who isn't. To separate the gold from the dross. The way I am, I want it all. I want someone honest and sincere and loyal and all that, and I want to be swept off my feet, too. He has to be the sexiest and the most exciting man in the world. I want to fall madly in love. I want to lose my head and my heart, the whole nine yards. Is that asking too much?"

Josh felt his gut twist into a knot. He was not that guy. He didn't have a chance with Bridget. Why did he think he did? Why did anybody think he did?

"No, it's not asking too much," he assured her. "You'll find him." But deep down he didn't want her to find him. He wanted her to stop looking.

It was almost dark now, but he saw her shake her head, turn away from him and unlatch the passenger door. Before he could get out and help her, she'd hopped out onto the sidewalk. She didn't thank him for the ride, she didn't say goodbye. She just left. He sat in his truck watching her.

Women. Would he ever understand them? They were having a discussion. He thought he was holding his end of it. But suddenly she left, leaving behind only her haunting scent and the smell of fresh-cut grass that clung to her clothes. He inhaled deeply and leaned back against the seat. What had made her jump out like a frightened rabbit? Was

it something he'd said? He turned his head and stared at
the window of the room above the shop, waiting for the
lights to go on. They never did. He drove around the block.
Then once more.

Bridget felt the tears coming way before Josh's com-
forting words, "You'll find him." He'd meant to be com-
forting, but he wasn't. What if she *had* found him, and he
didn't want to be found? She tossed her bag on the chair
and threw herself down on her bed and let the tears flow.
What had made her go on like that about the man she was
looking for?

Another minute in the truck with him and she would
have confessed *he* was the man she was looking for. She
got out just in time, because she was about to throw herself
at him and tell him she loved him. Which would have been
a big mistake. He would have been kind. He would have
been understanding. But it would have been awkward. Because Josh didn't love her, and he never would. Even if he
did, it didn't matter. He wasn't going to marry her or anybody else. Bridget admired the way he'd come out of his
"black hole" and into the world of the living. He was a
devoted father, a loving son and a wonderful brother. Those
were the some of the qualities that made him stand out from
other men. But dammit, why did she have to fall in love
with someone so outstanding, with so many assets, who
was totally out of her reach?

There was a knock on her door. Her heart pounded in
her chest. She switched on the bedside lamp and sat up so
suddenly she felt dizzy.

"Bridget, it's me," Josh said.

She took a deep breath, then she blew her nose, wiped
her eyes and got up and opened the door. For a long moment he stared down at her. She knew her eyes were red
and her hair was a mess. She was too strung out to care.

She didn't expect him. He should have been halfway home
by then. But he wasn't. He was there, filling her small room
with his broad shoulders, his large frame and his solid presence. Her heart sped up. Her knees wobbled. She should
say something like "come in," but her throat was dry, and
the words didn't come.

Why didn't *he* say something, instead of standing there
looking at her with that look he had? That look that asked
questions she couldn't answer.

Finally he did speak. "Can I come in?" he said.

"Oh, sure. Of course." The room wasn't that big, and it
suddenly got a lot smaller with Josh leaning against the
wall taking in the day bed, the desk and one overstuffed
chair. When his gaze returned to her, she wished for the
nth time that day that she hadn't worn the Western shirt
because of the way he was staring at it.

Self-consciously she tugged at the fringe.

"Did I tell you how much I like your shirt?"

"I...I don't think you did."

"Too bad about the stain."

"Oh, that's what you're staring at."

"I didn't do a very good job taking it out." He reached
out as if to try again, and she jerked back instinctively. If
he touched her again she'd be a basket case. She was just
on the edge, anyway.

"That's okay. Don't worry about it. I'll have it dry
cleaned. When I get home."

His eyes narrowed. "When will that be?"

"That depends. As soon as we finish shooting at your
place, I guess."

"You must find Harmony pretty dull. Here you are at
ten o'clock on a Friday night in a room over a shoe repair
store." He laughed mirthlessly. "What would you be doing
tonight if you were in San Francisco?"

She leaned against the arm of the chair. She knew what

he was thinking. That she was some kind of party girl, some big-city girl who could never be happy in a small town, who thought Harmony was the sticks. Okay, if that's what he thought, if that's what he wanted to think, she'd give him something to think about.

"Hmm, let me see," she mused, gazing off into space. "It's June, just in time for the opening of the opera. I guess I'd be at some sort of gala in one of my dozens of ball gowns. Dinner first at the Tonga Room. That's where *everyone* goes. Everyone who *is* anyone, that is. And after the opera, coffee on Union Street at one of those trendy little coffee houses. Just a hop, skip and a jump from my place in the Marina so after coffee—"

"That's enough," he said between clenched teeth. He grabbed her arm and yanked her out of her chair, bringing her up to face him.

Her eyes widened. "But you asked me. I thought you wanted to know," she said innocently.

He tightened his grip on her arm. "I changed my mind. I don't want to know about your dinners or your coffees or your ball gowns."

"You don't?" she asked. "You don't want to hear about my little black Versace or my fire-engine red Givenchy? Well, what do you want to hear about? What did you come up here for, anyway?"

His blue eyes glittered like ice. "You know what I came up here for." His gaze dropped to her breasts and the fringe that covered them. Covered them, but not well enough. Bridget could feel her nipples tighten and press against the soft white homespun cotton. And she knew that he was only too aware of the effect of his penetrating gaze.

Before she could come up with some smart remark, his eyes had gone from ice blue to hot burning flames of passion. The tremors started in her spine and spilled over into all the little nerve endings she hadn't known were exposed.

If he hadn't pulled her to him and held her like he'd never let her go, she would have fallen in a heap on the braid rug because her legs felt like rubber.

His lips captured hers in a fierce kiss. She staggered backward and they fell awkwardly onto the narrow bed together. He braced his elbows on the mattress. She arched forward to meet him halfway, but instead of meeting her lips in the torrid kiss she longed for, she yearned for, he stopped abruptly in midair.

"What's wrong?" she gasped, aching for his touch. Ready and waiting for the kisses that could scorch her soul.

"Wrong? We're wrong. You and me," he said, raising himself off the bed and standing above her. "You're ball gowns and opera galas, and I'm horses and dirt and wide-open spaces."

"I was teasing about the ball gowns," she said desperately, her cheeks burning.

"Yeah, right. You haven't got dozens, you've only got a few. It doesn't matter. What matters is you don't belong here. You're looking for a temporary diversion. And I'm not interested in a temporary diversion. I'm not interested in any kind of diversion. I've been trying to tell you that since the first day you got here. I have my life, and you have yours."

She sat on the edge of the bed, her hands pressed tightly together. "I know that, but—"

"Good. We both know that. And we both know enough to stay away from each other," he said, turning toward the door.

"Wait a minute," she said, getting to her feet, willing her trembling legs to hold her up. "I never thanked you for the ride, or said good-night."

"Good night," he said, and then he was gone.

Bridget didn't cry. She was cried out. She didn't sleep, either. She lay in her bed staring miserably at the ceiling as the minutes and the hours ticked by. What could she have said to make things better? What made him think she came from a different world than she did? The answers were "nothing" and "nothing." He thought what he thought and nobody could change his mind. She was a fool if she thought she could convince him she would fit into his life. Her latest attempt had just backfired. Royally. She would remember not to try sarcasm or exaggeration again. She'd remember not to try anything again. Not with Josh Gentry. She'd also remember to stay away from him as best she could.

After a sleepless night she came to the conclusion that although she wasn't destined to be anyone's wife or mother, she could succeed, with a little luck, as a top-flight advertising account executive, and she was going to make Wild Mustang men's cologne the hottest product of the year.

As a result, at the annual advertising awards ceremony in San Francisco next September, she was going to be standing on the stage accepting an award for most creative, most imaginative, sexiest TV commercial. She would beat out her former company, her former fiancé and everyone else in town. Yes, victory would be sweet, she told herself. And so would revenge against Scott. But would it be enough? Would it take the place of love?

Of course not, she told herself impatiently. But someday she'd have it all. Until then fame and fortune would just have to do. And the way to fame and fortune was to keep her cool, not let emotion get in the way of success, make the photo shoot the best she could—and get the hell out of town as soon as she could, without making a fool of herself by falling in love with the most unavailable man she'd ever come across. It sounded like a lot, but she could do it. She had to do it. She had no choice.

Chapter Nine

The film crew was scheduled to arrive at ten in the morning on Monday. Josh had been warned by a brief phone call from Bridget. He was feeling remorse ever since their encounter in her rented room, and he'd been forming an apology in his mind. But she didn't give him a chance to put it into words. He'd realized on his way home what mixed signals he'd been sending, coming on hot, then blowing cool, but on the phone she'd cut him off after telling him what to wear and what time to be ready. He vowed to make things right with her when he saw her, explain to her that she was the most attractive woman he'd seen in a long time, but...

But what? What if he'd given in to his instincts that night? He'd arrived at her door hot and bothered, ready to take whatever she'd give, but when she started blathering about her life in the city, it hit him all over again how really different they were and how impossible the situation was. And what a fool he'd been to even consider... What? A future with Bridget. It was ridiculous. She knew it as well as he did.

He wondered over and over what would have happened if he hadn't flown off the handle like that, if he'd kissed her senseless, then joined her in an escalating spiral of passion on that narrow little bed. What if they'd both peeled off their clothes, one by one, tossing them in a heap on the floor. He would have covered her body with his kisses until she was a sweet, sexy, overheated bundle of silk and velvet begging for him to fulfill her fantasies. She wouldn't have to beg. Just thinking about it still had him hot and bothered all over again, and breathing hard.

That wasn't the only reason he was bothered. After all these years of relative solitude, he was getting hooked on company—the company of his old friends and the company of one new friend. Her. He missed her when she wasn't around. So did Max. That went without saying. His son was restless and irritable, and still itchy. Josh felt exactly the same, and he hadn't even had chicken pox. He couldn't concentrate; the hours dragged; and he and Max were at each other's throats.

"Pick up your toys. The film crew will be here, and Bridget will be here, and the house is a mess."

"When, when will they be here?" Max demanded.

"Tomorrow, I told you."

"I'm bored," Max said.

"Bored? When I was your age—" He bit his tongue. When Josh was Max's age, he hated to have his parents nag him, and here he was behaving just the same way toward his son.

"Are they gonna take my picture, too?"

"Are you gonna smile?" Josh asked.

Max gave him a toothless smirk which made Josh smile for the first time in days. He ruffled the boy's hair. "That's it. They'll like that. Go practice some more smiles in the mirror. And when they see you, they won't be able to resist.

You'll be the Wild Mustang Boy.'' Josh certainly had a hard time resisting his son, especially since he'd been sick.

When the three-man crew finally arrived in their van behind Bridget's car, Max was an impatient basket case and Josh wasn't much better. It was just a photo shoot, he told himself. All he had to do was get on his horse and ride and let them worry about the rest. What if Bridget ignored him? He might have hurt her. He forced himself to stop pacing back and forth.

Josh watched while the crew, all long-haired artistic types in stiff new jeans and wraparound sunglasses, piled out of their van and stared at the vast open spaces, the dusty red earth and the bare distant hills as if they were in the valley of the moon. While they unloaded their equipment, Max ran headlong for Bridget, threw his arms around her knees and almost knocked her over.

"Hey," she said lifting him up in her arms. "Let me look at you. Are you all better now?

"Yep. I got rid of my pox and I'm all better. Can I get my picture taken, too? Dad said I gotta smile. Like this.'' Josh couldn't see his face, but he could imagine the same smirk Max had been practicing for two days.

Bridget laughed and looked over Max's head at Josh. When her gaze met his, the familiar world around him faded away. The red soil and the distant hills and the wide-open sky all blended together. His heart pounded. He rocked back on the heels of his boots and caught his breath, as if he'd never seen her before. God, she was beautiful with the sun picking up gold highlights in her hair and the laughter on her lips.

"Sure you can, tiger," she said, turning her gaze back to Max. "They brought plenty of film. You can even take some pictures if you want. I told them you already know how. First I've got to get my groceries out of my car. I'm making dinner for you all tonight.''

"I'll help," he said without Josh even reminding him. Josh offered to help, too, but Bridget said she and Max could manage. Instead he went to the barn to check on the horse he was planning to ride today. For the umpteenth time. He came out just as Max and Bridget emerged from the house.

Max was tugging at Bridget's hand. "Let's go take some more pictures of you acting silly. You gotta do some more songs and dances 'cuz my dad laughed so hard when he saw you."

"Oh, he did, did he?" Bridget asked, walking slowly toward the fence with Max at her side. Josh had settled on the top bar of the fence, bracing himself with his arms outstretched along the rail.

"Oh, yeah, he watched so many times he 'bout wore out that videotape you gave me."

Josh could have cheerfully throttled the boy. He didn't want Bridget to know he'd sat up half the night watching her and many nights since. She might think he'd lost his mind. Or his heart. He didn't know which he could more easily do without, his mind or his heart. He shot his son a warning look, but Max just giggled.

"So you laughed at my singing and dancing, did you?" she asked Josh with her hands on her hips. "I'm glad I provided you with so much entertainment. But that was nothing. If I'd known you were going to watch I would have enlarged my repertoire. I could have done better. I wasn't really trying. I didn't know you'd be watching."

"Hey, you were great," Josh said, relieved by her light-hearted attitude. For all he knew he'd hurt her feelings irreparably. But she'd bounced back as if that night had never happened. "Especially that teacup song. How did it go? Tip me over and pour me out." He leaned forward, over the fence, to demonstrate, and Bridget, to Max's delight, reached up with both hands and pushed him off the fence onto the ground.

"If I didn't know better," he said, slowly picking himself off the rust-red soil and brushing the dirt off his pants, "I'd say you were jealous. I'd say *you* want to be the Wild Mustang *Woman*." He walked up to her, his finger pointed at her chest, stopping only inches from the cleft between her breasts. "That's it, isn't it? You're not going to stop at a *men's* cologne, you're going to have women smelling like horses, too. And you're going to be the symbol. You, a city girl, are going to take over. To win fame and fortune. Am I right?" he asked, tapping her lightly on the chest.

Palms forward as if to protect herself, Bridget backed away, while Max leaned against the fence, gleefully watching the adult antics, astounded to see his father acting so silly. It was better than a cartoon. Better than a movie. He knew Bridget could let her hair down, he had the video to prove it, but his father, his serious, hardworking father…well, that was another matter.

"That's ridiculous," she said. "Although now that you mention it, it's not a bad idea."

"That's why you bought that shirt with the fringe, isn't it? Now all you need is a hat and boots to go with it."

Bridget's face turned scarlet. She choked back a retort.

"You didn't. Did you?" he asked. He turned to Max. "How would you like to see Bridget in a whole Western getup?"

"In boots and everything?" He bobbed his head up and down. "That'd be cool. I'll take her picture." Then he dashed off to watch the crew unload their gear.

Bridget watched him go. "Okay, I'll bring my outfit to show you tomorrow, if you promise not to laugh. It'll be my last day."

"What?" Josh said, startled.

"If all goes well, they'll be finished shooting tomorrow.

I certainly wouldn't want to take any more of your time," she said.

Josh stared at her. He knew she'd leave soon, but not this soon. Tomorrow was her last day. He couldn't believe it. He felt like he'd been thrown off his wild mustang on his butt. Dazed. Shaken up.

"I didn't know," he blurted. "I mean, I knew you were leaving, but... Max doesn't know. I don't know how to tell him. He's going to miss you."

She nodded. "I'll tell him. I'm going to miss him, too. Come and meet the crew," she said. "We should get started."

She seemed so cool, so matter-of-fact. But what did he expect after their last meeting? Still, it was hard for him to accept that this was just another job for her. It would be even harder for a five-year-old whose mother had died. If she didn't care about Josh, couldn't she have some feeling for his son? Josh heard her say the names of the photographers but promptly forgot them. He shook hands with them, tried to look them in the eye, but all he saw was his haggard-looking face reflected in their sunglasses. Then they all set out for a tour of the property.

Josh took the lead; Max followed close behind him, half skipping, half running in an effort to keep up, proudly wearing a camera on a strap around his neck. Bridget walked along with the crew who were carrying their tripods, reflectors and minicams, giving a running commentary and instructions.

"A silhouette...different backgrounds...profile...macho sexy symbol...."

Josh was still in a state of shock. Leaving. She was leaving. Without thinking, he automatically saddled the horse he'd chosen, one he'd tamed and trained a year ago. He made a few circles around the corral so the crew could get a sense of what they wanted. Then he walked his horse to the top of the hill, the crew following slowly and panting at the unaccustomed exercise, where Bridget suggested certain angles and certain shots. The photographers nodded, they made notes, and they made marks on the ground with chalk.

Josh put the horse through the motions. Rearing back on his hind legs. Racing over the hill. Tossing his head, his mane flowing in the wind. Well trained, it did exactly what the crew wanted with a minimum of commands from Josh. Which was fortunate, because Josh's mind was unable to focus on horsemanship. His mind and his eyes wandered to Bridget and then to Max. He should have prepared his son for this. He'd told him she would leave sometime, but not when. When was she going to tell him? When, when, when?

Next they went back to the corral, and Josh did a few rope tricks from his saddle just to see if he still could, and the photographers loved it. They poked their heads through the slats of the fence to catch his act from all angles. They let Max snap pictures, too. They very generously let him sit on their shoulders and look through their viewfinder. They held him up in the air over their heads. He was beaming with pride.

That was Bridget's doing, he thought, watching him focus his camera in an effort to be just like the professionals. She'd primed them to be nice to him. She wanted this to be a good experience for Max. A memorable experience. It would be. But it wouldn't make it any easier for him to accept the fact that she was leaving.

It wasn't quite true, as Bridget had said, that the photographers would work around him, that he could pose on his horse for a few minutes and then continue to do his normal work. He hadn't really ever believed that, but only now did he realize how long it took them to get the perfect shot. How often they'd repeat the same action, over and over.

He should have known what a perfectionist Bridget would be.

When they broke for lunch, he was tired of doing the same routine over and over and ready to go back to being a wild horse trainer. The crew brought a cooler full of beer and soft drinks to the picnic table behind the house, and Bridget went to her car for the ice chest containing the large meat and cheese sandwiches she'd ordered from the diner in town.

"I want a shot of horse and rider on the hill outlined against the sunset," Bridget told the crew between bites of her sandwich. "Sunsets here are beautiful."

"What about sunrise?" Josh asked. "Sunrises can be spectacular."

"Sunrise. I never thought of that," Bridget mused, as she took a swig of cola from the can. "Would you mind getting up that early?" she asked Josh.

"No, but would you? You'd have to stay overnight."

Oh, Lord. Not overnight. Not in his house, his beautiful, comfortable house where she felt so much at home. Too much at home. But what could she say? She was afraid to stay there for fear of forming an attachment? Which was a little like closing the barn door after the horse had escaped. She couldn't give up the most spectacular photo opportunity of her career because she couldn't trust herself to sleep under the same roof as Josh.

They'd been through this before. It was déjà vu all over again. She'd made dinner in his kitchen, she'd been ready to spend the night, then fate had intervened when his in-laws called and she left. Who would call tonight, what would prevent her from spending her last night in Harmony under Josh's roof? Who or what would save her from temptation? It had to be something, because this was the worst idea she'd ever heard.

This kind of temptation—the temptation to pretend she

was part of the family—was too hard to resist. What if no one called. What if she was forced into sleeping under his roof, or worse, *not* sleeping under his roof, lying there staring at the ceiling thinking about him?

What if in the middle of the night she got up off the couch or the futon and went and knocked on his door and threw herself at him, begged him to make love to her before she left town? No, she didn't trust herself. Better to head it off. Better not to stay there. "You already have a houseful," she said. "I can't take advantage of your hospitality. I'll go back to town tonight and come back early in the morning. Before sunrise."

"Stay here," he said firmly, reaching across the picnic table to cover her hand with his. "Stay here with us."

It wasn't an invitation, it was an order. She was so startled she couldn't speak. She looked around. The crew had wandered off to have a cigarette.

"I don't understand you," she said. "The last time I saw you you said—"

"I know what I said," he said in a low tone. "And I'm sorry. I should never have come up to your room, and once I did, I never should have left. I can't tell you how much I've regretted it."

"Coming up or leaving?" she asked.

"Both. But what's done is done. If you're afraid I'll come on to you again, don't be. All I'm concerned with is your future. Your happiness. Your job. Your success. I want you to stay here so you'll get the best shots in the morning. So you won't miss a minute of the action." Just for a second she wondered if he was talking about more action than the sun rising in the east. Though his words were earnest, there was a certain look in his eyes that caused her knees to knock together under the table.

Fortunately he couldn't see under the table. All he saw was the casual shrug of the shoulders as if it didn't matter

one way or the other where she spent her last night in
Harmony. But it did. Oh, yes, it did. Before she could say
anything else Josh had turned to answer one of the photog-
rapher's questions about panning for gold in Nevada's river
beds.

Max was ecstatic when he heard Bridget was staying all
night. He was also exhausted from running around all
morning. So tired that when Bridget volunteered to take
him in for a nap after lunch he didn't even put up a fight.
She tucked him into his bed, wondering if this was the time
to tell him she was leaving. Watching his eyes close, one
little hand still holding hers, she knew she couldn't do it.

Especially when he asked her just before he drifted off,
"You'll be here when I wake up, won't you Bridget?"

"Sure I will. I'll be here all day tomorrow, and then..."

Even if she'd had the courage to tell him, which she
didn't, he was asleep. With one last look at him, she closed
the door behind her and went back outside. There she found
Max wasn't the only one who was tired. The cameramen
were ready for their naps, too. They'd made it as far as the
cottonwood tree in the front yard before they collapsed on
their backs under its leafy shade to digest their lunch.

"So much for your crew," Josh said "One morning in
Harmony and they've passed out."

"This would never happen in San Francisco," Bridget
said, staring at the supine bodies on the grass. "It must be
the heat."

"So Max didn't even protest?" Josh asked.

"Not a bit. Fell asleep immediately," she said.

"You and I are the only ones left standing," he noted.

Bridget met his gaze for just a moment. What would he
do if she said she didn't want to be left standing? That she
wanted to send everyone away and lie on the warm grass
in his arms, dreamily staring up at the branches of the ju-
niper trees. She wanted to make love with him under those

trees, to see the dappled sun on his sun-bronzed body. To feel the grass tickle her bare legs, to breathe in the smell of his hair and his skin, to feel his mouth on hers.

What was wrong with her? He'd made it clear to her they had no future. She was at work, in the middle of a project. Yes, it must be the heat. Or Harmony. Or Josh. Or all three.

She blinked to clear her mind of these subversive thoughts. She looked at her watch. She called to the crew. They stretched, got to their feet and shot reams of videotape and film all afternoon, until sunset when they finally got the shot Bridget knew was going to be the one. The sky was a palette of orange and crimson. Josh and his horse made a stunning picture outlined against the sky. It was all there—power, strength, sex appeal. Bridget licked her dry lips and remembered that first moment she'd seen him. That magic moment when she knew he was the one. The Wild Mustang Man.

She heaved a sigh of relief. Whatever happened, whatever came of this trip to this remote corner of Nevada, she'd gotten what she came for. She'd gotten more than that. So much more. No, she couldn't let herself think about how hot the sun felt at high noon on Main Street in downtown Harmony, how dusk fell over the ranch, throwing shadows over the pasture, how Max's little hand felt in hers, and how those things would be only memories after tomorrow.

She forced herself to think about dinner. This was not the time to reflect on her experiences in Harmony. She couldn't afford to start feeling melancholy about leaving. Before she could sink into that morass she hustled into the kitchen and while the crew took turns in the shower and Max watched TV, she constructed a casserole with the broccoli, chicken, rice and sour cream she'd bought in town. It was one she'd made before at home, so she didn't have to concentrate too hard—fortunately, because her mind kept wandering, thinking of tomorrow. Tomorrow, her last day.

When she looked up, Josh was standing in the doorway, fresh from the shower, his damp hair hanging over his forehead, wearing clean jeans, a polo shirt and bare feet—exuding power, strength and sex appeal. She knew how he'd smell if she went up and brushed his hair back from his forehead, then linked her arms around his neck and nuzzled her face against his neck. He'd smell like soap and leather and clean clothes and not a hint of cologne, Wild Mustang or any other. He didn't need any.

He was sexy enough as he was. More than enough. For a moment she was struck with doubts about the necessity of a men's cologne. But all men weren't as sexy as Josh. Some men could use a little help. Those men could use a little Wild Mustang men's cologne. With a huge effort, she tore her eyes away from his broad shoulders and tapered hips

"I was wrong about your being able to go about your work while we took pictures of you. We've taken up your whole day, and I apologize," she said, opening the oven door to check on the chicken.

He shrugged. "I suspected as much. I planned for it. Tomorrow, too. Don't worry about it. I'll have plenty of time to work after you leave."

After she left. It was obvious he could hardly wait until she left so he could get back to work. He'd made that clear to her since the first day she'd arrived. It shouldn't still hurt so much to hear it again. "The shots of you and your horse against the sky all orange and red were really beautiful," she said, leaning back against the counter. "I don't see how we could do any better in the morning."

"Then you don't want to get up for sunrise?" he asked, stacking dinner plates on the table.

"Oh sure, of course. If I don't, I'd always wonder what

if." As if she wasn't going to wonder *what if* about other things. *What if* she told Josh she loved him, that she'd stay here forever if he asked her? That she'd…she'd…what would she do here in the middle of nowhere when her life was back in the city? Nothing. How long would she last? About ten minutes, according to Kate.

But what about the way she felt here on the ranch, out in the corral or the pasture, inside the warmth of the kitchen, with Max's arms around her knees? Or what about Josh's sexy teasing banter? What about it? she asked herself. It adds up to nothing. Nothing she could count on. Nothing but a brief fling. Nothing but a brief working vacation where she had learned more about life and love and herself in a matter of weeks than she'd learned in years. And now it was over. Or it would be tomorrow.

While Josh answered questions over dinner about Nevada's climate, geography and history, the crew dug into Bridget's chicken divan casserole, salad and ice cream sundaes with huge appetites. So did Max and Josh when they weren't too busy talking about ranch life, about how Max had made a bike trail all the way to his grandparents' house and how Josh had been training wild mustangs since he was old enough to sit in a saddle.

After dinner the crew went out to smoke cigarettes on the front porch. Max followed them and Josh and Bridget cleaned up the kitchen.

"I've worked with these guys before," Bridget said, filling the sink with soapy water. "I've never seen them so interested in anything as they are in your way of life. Usually they're pretty blasé."

"Do you always cook for them?" Josh asked. "Put them up overnight?"

"Oh, no. We've never gone this far afield on location. It's quite an experience for them. They must feel like they're in another world. I do."

"Looking forward to getting back to your real world?" he asked, pausing at the dish cabinet.

"Of course," she said a little too quickly. "But I've had a wonderful time here."

"You don't have to be polite, Bridget. Harmony must seem like a backwater. I understand."

She let that go. She wasn't going to tell him that she'd never felt so welcome anywhere. That she'd gotten hooked on the fresh air and the wide-open spaces and the nice people. She even liked the dry heat and the sagebrush.

"Ever been to San Francisco?" she asked.

"Nope," he said leaning against the counter.

"Maybe you'll come for the introduction of the cologne in the fall."

"Fall's a busy time for me."

"You don't have to be polite, Josh. Just say you're not interested. I understand."

"Okay, I'm not interested. I told you before how I felt about men's cologne. I'm not much for cities, either."

She stacked the last dish firmly in the rack and turned around. "How do you know if you've never been there? You might be surprised. I never thought I'd like Harmony so much, but I do. I'm not being polite, either."

"Whatever you say," he said, observing her through narrowed eyes.

At that point she didn't care if he believed her or not. One more day. Just one more day and then she'd be gone. He'd be glad to get back to his real life. But would she?

"I'm going to put Max to bed now," Josh said. "He's not going to like that. He doesn't want to miss any more excitement. Especially after he was forced to take a nap."

"I didn't force him. I didn't have to. He gave up. He let me know, however, that he wasn't a baby."

Josh nodded. "Well, I already gave the crew the guest room, so I'm afraid you draw the couch in the living room.

Blankets and pillow are in the closet,'' he said before he turned and left the room.

She bit her lip, surprised and a little hurt he'd dismissed her so brusquely. When would they say goodbye, or wouldn't they? Tomorrow, at the end of the day, would she just drive off into the sunrise with a casual wave? That was probably better than some teary embrace. "See you at sunrise," she called. "And Josh...thanks again for your hospitality. We couldn't have done it without you. I know you didn't want me here, but—"

"Forget it," he said over his shoulder. He was clearly uncomfortable with her sincere gratitude. Probably afraid she was going to launch into some emotional discussion with him. But she had to say something, and it was better said now than later. She went into the living room, found the pillow and blanket and tossed them on the extra-long leather couch. Dimming all the lights but one small desk lamp with a cowhide shade, she stretched on the couch and observed the native American wall hangings and rugs that had so impressed her that first day, trying to forget tomorrow was her last day.

On the mantel above the stone fireplace was a pair of silver candlesticks and next to them the large photograph of Molly, with her soft eyes and her sweet smile. She seemed to be looking straight at Bridget. Welcoming her to Harmony, to her house, to the living room she'd so carefully furnished. Bridget remembered hearing her friends describe her as a saint, and the way her picture was positioned between the candles almost reminded her of a shrine. What would she say if she knew Bridget had fallen in love with her husband and her son?

If she really was a saint, she might say, "Josh needs a wife, Bridget. His family is right. Just because I died first doesn't mean he's supposed to stay single the rest of his life. And Max definitely needs a mother. You're not quite

what I had in mind, you know, a career girl and a city girl
to boot, but I believe you have potential. You seem to be
fond of Josh. I was. He was the only man I ever loved. If
you think you can make him happy, go for it."

"Go for it...how?" Bridget murmured. "He's as good
as told me I don't have a chance. Nobody does. Nobody
can compete with you. Especially not me. I don't grow
vegetables or make my own jam or roam the county taking
care of other people in trouble."

"What about Max?" Molly asked in Bridget's mind.
"You took care of him when he was sick."

"Yes, but..."

"The jam isn't important. Oh, sure, winning first prize
at the county fair was a thrill. One of my wishes that came
true. Make your own wishes, Bridget. Find a lucky star and
make a wish. Then make it come true."

"Is that how it works?" Bridget asked. "Is that how you
got everything you wanted? A husband who adored you,
who still adores you and a little boy and—" A sigh of pure
envy escaped her lips, and she turned her head toward the
landscape paintings of red rocks and desert on the far wall.

Her eyelids drooped. She was tired, physically and mentally exhausted, but when she turned out the light, she
couldn't sleep. It was too early, that was the problem. Too
early to go to bed, too late to stay up, and nowhere to go.
She couldn't risk running into Josh and starting another
awkward conversation. She heard footsteps in the hall,
Josh's. Voices, belonging to the crew. Max's voice calling
his father to bring him a glass of water. She pictured the
little boy sitting up in bed reaching out for the glass, his
lively brain thinking up more excuses to put off the inevitable bedtime.

She stared out the large, picture window at the starry
night. Was there a wishing star out there for her? She tossed
off the wool blanket with the geometric Indian design, got

up and went to the window. There were too many stars, and she had too many wishes. And it was too late. Tomorrow night she'd be on the road, back to San Francisco. Back home.

She pressed her forehead against the window. Home. Once she got there she'd be fine. She'd been away too long already. She'd started to think of this corner of the world as home. She'd adjusted to this arid landscape, this small town, these friendly people, faster than she could have imagined.

When she got home, she would plunge herself back into work. She had plenty to do, tying up this Wild Mustang business. Then she had to find another account. Her fragile new business couldn't rely on one men's cologne account, no matter how popular and lucrative it became. She had to get out there and hustle. To show everyone, including one Scott Marsten and his father's company that she was not a one-account agency.

"Bridget. What is it? What's out there?"

She whirled around to see Josh standing in the semi-darkness of the living room.

"The stars. I was thinking of making a wish, but I don't know which star it is I'm supposed to wish on."

"Sometimes it's better not to make a wish," he said walking to the window to look out with her. "What do they say? Be careful what you wish for, it might come true."

There was such sadness in his voice, Bridget stared at him in surprise. It was too dark to read the expression in his eyes. In the moonlight they were only deep pools of hidden meaning. She could only guess at the grief he felt, even now, at the wish that ended too soon. But did he wish he could take back his wish?

"What do you mean?" she asked. "I thought..."

"You thought my wish came true. Yes, I got married to

Molly." He turned to look at her picture on the mantel. Though Bridget couldn't make out her features from there, Josh must know them by heart. "It was all I ever wanted. That and making my living here on the ranch. But we were only eighteen, too young to know what we really wanted. So we got married. And found out we wanted different things.

"Molly wanted to have children. Right away. She was a great nurturer. A wonderful mother when it finally happened. But it didn't happen for a long time. A long frustrating time for her while she tried to get pregnant. As an alternative, she devoted herself to helping the people in the community. If there was an emergency, Molly was there. A sick child, an accident in the field, a friend in the hospital—she was on the scene with her homemade bread, her jam and her tireless nurturing."

"She'd be gone for days sometimes. The gratitude she got, the love she felt for the community, and the appreciation, somewhat made up for the lack of a child in her life. But not entirely. Just taking care of the house and me wasn't enough. I knew that. I understood, but I didn't know what to do, how to help her. The harder we tried to have a baby, the harder it was to conceive, and the more frustrated we got. We couldn't talk about it. But we thought about it all the time. At least she did. She said she didn't blame me. But I felt like I'd failed her, anyway."

Bridget took a step backward and bumped into the arm of the overstuffed chair that flanked the window. Her knees wobbled so much she could no longer stand. Her hands were ice-cold. She didn't know what to say. That Josh would confide in her this way overwhelmed her. To find out that his perfect marriage was not perfect shocked her to the core.

"What did you do?" she asked.

"Do? I bought wild mustangs. I broke them, I trained

them and I sold them. I became one of the best around here. I didn't complain. How could I? I'd gotten everything I'd wished for. But I sometimes wondered if I should have gone to college, like Jed did. Learned something about agribusiness, more than my dad could teach me. Or studied art, literature, what have you. That sounds crazy, doesn't it?''

"No, not at all. I think at our age everyone has second thoughts or some regrets just wondering *what if.* I guess you were a little young, but maybe you were having a sort of midlife crisis. Anyway things must have changed when Max was born.''

"Yes, oh, yes. Molly was consumed with Max. And she still made time for everyone else who needed her. Everyone but me.''

"What?''

"I've never told anyone about this. I don't know why I'm telling you now.''

"Maybe because I'm a stranger. I have no ties to Harmony, and I'm leaving tomorrow.''

"That must be it,'' he said. "Anyway, I don't mean to complain about Molly. She was perfect. The perfect wife and mother and neighbor. That's what everyone said. And then she died. Before I could tell her how I felt about her. How much I loved her, appreciated what she'd done. What she'd made of herself.''

"But she knew. She must have known,'' Bridget said. "For her you were the perfect husband. Just as she was the perfect wife.''

"I don't understand it. How could God take anyone so good?'' Josh asked, his face contorted with anger. He pounded his fist against the woodwork. "How could He take Max's mother away from him?''

Bridget's eyes filled with tears. She stood and crossed the floor and put her arms around him, feeling his solid muscles. "Maybe we're not meant to understand," she said. "Maybe we just have to accept that."

Josh closed the gap between them and ran his hands down her back and buried his face in her hair. He was drained. He'd never meant to tell her. He'd never meant to tell anybody. Was it really because she was leaving tomorrow? Because she had nothing to do with him or his life? Or was it because she understood? That she knew him better than those who had known him all his life?

The heat from her body warmed him, the understanding she felt came through in a wave of overwhelming, heart-wrenching emotion that rocked his body and yet gave him strength. Over her head he glanced up at the framed photo of his wife. His former wife. His late wife. For the first time he thought of her in the past without feeling guilty.

He tilted Bridget's chin to look at her. Moonlight gilded her face and turned her hair to spun sugar. In her eyes he saw tiny embers of desire flickering in the moonlight. Desire rocketed through him like a tornado, making him want to fan those embers, bring them to flaming passion. It was madness. He'd just finished telling her about his marriage and his former wife, and suddenly he'd been set free. Free from guilt and betrayal. And now all he could think about, all he could feel was a surge of relief and Bridget. Bridget in his mind and in his heart and in his arms.

He kissed her, and she kissed him back. Her touch, her scent, inflamed him. His tongue slid between her parted lips, seeking, thrusting, savoring. He could finally admit to himself that Bridget's kisses did things to him that no one else's ever had. Made him want her in a way he'd never wanted anyone before. He marveled at how her body molded to his, her breasts pressed against his chest, her hips locked against his.

It was happening again. Every time he kissed her it happened. Every time she kissed him. Needs swirled around them like tumbleweed, catching at their clothes, threatening to sweep them away in a tide of passion. He didn't want to love Bridget. He didn't want to love anyone, and he didn't want anyone to love him. Not like that. Because he was never going to get married again. He couldn't risk losing the person he loved.

But he did love her. More than he thought possible. Because if this wasn't love…he didn't know what was.

He kissed her over and over, filling his mouth with the taste of her. The little sounds she made in the back of her throat urged him on. Made his heart hammer. He wanted to leave his imprint on her, so she'd remember him—at least for a while. He'd never forget her. He knew that. But her life was exciting, fast paced, filled with people and events. There was no room for him in it. There was plenty of room for her in his life, but she'd never be happy there. Never. What if he told her he loved her right now and she turned him down? He would never get over it. What if by some miracle, she married him and he lost her the way he'd lost Molly? No, he couldn't take that chance.

Finally, with all the willpower he could muster, he took her by the shoulders and held her at arm's length. She was only a few inches away, but far enough to let him catch his breath…to see the dazed expression in her eyes, her kiss-swollen lips in the moonlight.

"Good night, Bridget," he said. Then, before he could change his mind, he turned on his heel and went down the hall to his room.

Chapter Ten

Sunrise is a magical time, Bridget thought, scanning the horizon. Even in the city. Watching the sun come up over the Bay from the window of her tiny apartment always filled her with awe. But as she stepped out the front door of the ranch house, in the hush of morning, with the sun peeking over the distant mountains, she felt as if she was witnessing a miracle. For a few moments she forgot her worry about telling Max goodbye, forgot the sad fact that she was leaving for good, forgot her fatigue from staying awake half the night tossing and turning and trying to understand what was happening to her life.

She walked through the long, lush, dewy grass unaware that her shoes were soaked through. She could see the crew in the distance already setting up to take advantage of the perfect moment. In a few minutes Josh would be on the hill outlined against the sunrise, his horse rearing, its mane tossed in the wind. Right now he was leading his horse out of the barn, his head down, talking softly to the animal. She watched them come toward her, both horse and man unaware of her presence. How she envied Josh's life here, his peaceful existence, his ability to do what he loved, without pressure, among friends and relatives. Most of all she envied him his son. He looked up, saw Bridget and stopped abruptly.

"Sleep all right?" he asked gruffly. She felt his gaze rake her body, and self-consciously she smoothed her wrinkled shirt and ran a hand through her tousled hair.

A shiver ran up her spine. It could have been her wet shoes, but it was more likely the look in his eyes, the hunger she saw there, the out-and-out temptation she recognized because it matched her own. His deep resonant voice alone was all it took to send goose bumps up and down her arms.

"Great," she lied, with what she hoped was a perky smile. "How are you?"

"Couldn't be better," he said.

She doubted that. There were lines etched in his forehead that hadn't been there yesterday and a tightening in the muscles around his mouth. Memories of the words spoken last night—and the one *not* spoken—hovered in the air between them. Tension crackled in the air that just a few moments ago had been serene. He tightened his grip on the reins.

"Well, I guess we're about ready," she said, glancing at the crew, fighting off the desire to fasten the buttons on his vest, to straighten the collar of his checkered cotton shirt and run her fingers through his unruly hair. If it had been anyone else, some random male model she'd paid to do the job, she wouldn't have hesitated. But with Josh she couldn't trust herself to touch him, even in the name of improving his image. Not even with one little finger. Not after last night. Not ever again.

He nodded and swung into the saddle so effortlessly she wished she had a picture of that, just that. Not that she'd ever forget how he looked on a horse, as if the animal was an extension of himself, all sinew and grace in motion. She would have enough pictures of Josh Gentry, there'd be one on every bottle of cologne, on every cosmetic counter, billboard, print ad...yes, she'd have no trouble remembering him. Just the opposite. She was going to have trouble forgetting him.

She couldn't bear to break the morning silence by yelling orders to the crew, so she waved to them and trusted they'd do what they had to do. By the time she'd trudged up the hill, the silver and pink streaks were fading from the sky, the pale moon was setting and they were folding their tripods.

The rest of the day went just as smoothly, as the crew went around taking one more round of pictures. "Insurance film," they called it, just to be sure they had enough.

"Wouldn't want to have to come back here," one of the photographers said after the lunch break.

"Why not?" Bridget asked with a frown. She was as offended as if he'd insulted her personally. Which was crazy. This wasn't her home, her ranch, her town. After today she'd never see it again.

"You know," he said with a wave at the wide-open spaces that surrounded the ranch. "It's so...empty. Nothing to do here."

Nothing to do but live. A different life, yes, but one that suited the inhabitants of Harmony very well, so well she was half-envious of them. Josh disappeared into the barn with his horse. The crew was packing their gear into their van. Time was running out. Bridget knew she couldn't put off telling Max she was leaving any longer.

She walked through the front door as she'd done that very first day. glancing at Molly's picture on the mantel as she passed, wondering if she'd had a chance to say goodbye to her son. Unlike Molly, Bridget knew nothing about chil-

dren. Had no idea how to say goodbye or how to tell him
she was leaving. She wiped her damp palms on her blue
jeans as she walked down the hall. Her feet felt like they
were made of lead as she dragged them across the wide-
planked floor. Maybe she was making too big a deal out
of this. Maybe she was transferring her own feelings onto
a five-and-a-half-year-old child.

Max was sprawled on his stomach on the floor of his
room, building a structure of Lego blocks.

"Hey," she said, getting down on her knees, "how're
you doing?"

"Makin' a motocross," he said, grabbing a model mo-
torcycle with one hand and pushing it over a Lego-built
bridge. "Zoooom," he yelled, as the toy sailed through the
air and crashed into Bridget's arm.

"Aaaaaah," she said, drawing back with mock terror.

He grinned, showing the gaps between his baby teeth.
"Just like the time I crashed into you the first day you
came, remember?" he asked.

"I remember." She took a deep breath. "That was the
first day, and now today…" Oh, Lord, give her strength to
say this. "Today is the last day. I have to go home today."

He wrinkled his freckled nose. "Where's your home?"

"My home…" She looked around his room, at the beige
walls covered with posters and lined with shelves holding
his prized and precious belongings. To her, home was a
rented apartment. To him and to generations of Gentrys this
ranch was home and always would be. He took it for
granted. He was too young to realize what a gift that was.

"My home is in San Francisco," she continued. "It's a
big city in California. If I leave today in my car I'll be
home tomorrow. That's how far away it is."

"When are you coming back?" he asked solemnly, looking up at her with the trademark Gentry blue eyes.

She blinked rapidly. She must not cry. She would not

cry. "Well...I'm probably not coming back. See, I have a job there. I came here..."

"I know, you came here to buy a horse. That's what you said, didn't you?" he asked, scratching his arm.

"Yes...no. I didn't mean that. I meant I came to see your dad about a horse but what I wanted was for him to have his picture taken *riding* a horse. His horse. That's what we've been doing. Taking pictures. You know because you've been helping."

"I was a big help, wasn't I?"

She smiled and ruffled his blond hair. "Yes you were. And when I get back, I'm going to send you the pictures. The ones of you and the ones you took. You could pin them on your bulletin board. Would you like that?"

Instead of the enthusiastic response she expected, he lowered his head and averted her gaze. "I guess so," he mumbled.

Oh, no. If he cried, if he even sounded like he might cry, she was going to cry, too. If she wanted to leave with any shred of dignity, she had to leave now. She couldn't risk hugging him or she might never leave at all.

"Goodbye, Max," she said over the lump in her throat. She jumped to her feet and ran out the door before either one of them broke down. Walking briskly toward the front door, her eyes blinded with unshed tears, she told herself he'd be fine. He had everything he needed right here. So if she wasn't crying for Max, who was she crying for?

She almost ran into Josh on the front steps. She managed a watery smile and backed up onto the porch. "I...we're almost finished, I guess, so...I said goodbye to Max."

"Oh." That was all he said. But his eyes, such a dark blue they looked almost black, bored into hers. The next question hung in the air, unspoken. What about him? What about saying goodbye to Josh?

She swallowed hard. "Before I go, I just want to say

that I appreciate everything you've done. I know you didn't want to do this, posing for pictures for two days. But I hope it hasn't been too painful. In any case, you'll get a check just as soon as—''

"I didn't do it for the money," he said.

"I know, but…why *did* you do it?" she asked, leaning against the wooden railing, her forehead etched with faint lines. If she didn't ask now, she'd never know.

He shrugged. "I don't know. Curious, maybe." He gave her a long, penetrating look that rattled her so much she had to knot her hands together so they wouldn't tremble.

"About Wild Mustang cologne? I'll send you the first bottle off the production line."

"That's not what I meant. I was curious about you."

"You mean what was a nice girl like me doing in the wicked, cutthroat advertising business?" she asked lightly.

"I mean what was a nice girl like you doing in my bathroom?"

"Well, now you know." She told herself this conversation was going nowhere. She told herself to say goodbye and leave. But she just stood there staring down at him from the porch, wishing she knew what to say, wanting to leave, longing to stay, wishing he'd tell her to stay, but knowing he wouldn't.

In the end she brushed past him, intensely aware of the heat from his body, the earthy smell of leather mingled with the musky, male scent of Josh Gentry that could never be captured in a bottle. If it could, women would be lined up around the block waiting for a chance to pay fifty dollars an ounce for it. She mumbled incoherently something about being in touch with him. On the way to her car in the driveway, she spoke to the crew about what route to take back to San Francisco or maybe it was about the price of hay. A few minutes later she had no idea what she'd said.

She drove to town, picked up her belongings, paid the

rent and drove away. Watching the town disappear in her rearview mirror, she saw the one-story, sand-colored buildings get smaller until they faded away in the dust, saw the whole town swallowed up as if it had never been there. As if she'd never sat in the diner drinking coffee with Suzy and Tally, or bought clothes for the party at the dry goods store, or made phone calls to the Gentry Ranch from the pay phone on the corner.

It was over.... She kept telling herself until the words had burned a pattern in her brain. Over. Over. Over. Until the tears stopped falling. Somewhere around the state line.

The next week was difficult for Josh. The week after that even more so. He found himself staring out the kitchen window, letting the canned soup boil over on the stove, as he remembered the night he and Max taught Bridget to work a slingshot. Instead of paying bills in his den, he picked up a pad of paper and started a letter to Bridget. There was so much he wanted to say. Things he couldn't say in person. About how much she'd changed his life. How she'd made him see things in a way he never had before. How she'd made him feel things he never dreamed possible. Explaining that even if he were free to love again, he couldn't afford to take a chance on losing the woman he loved. It had been too painful last time. It had taken a Herculean effort to get his life back on keel. He'd made that effort for Max's sake.

What about Max? He couldn't afford to lose another mother. This was something Josh had never told Bridget, never even consciously thought about before. Because there was no reason to articulate it. It was simply there. He and Max were in no condition to risk their hard-won stability by taking a chance on another woman in their lives. They were better off by themselves. This fact was a part of him, a part of what made him what he was.

But after he'd scrawled "Dear Bridget" on the paper, he dropped his pen and was lost in a blur of memories. Bridget's determined expression across the fifty-yard line playing touch football, Bridget at the horse auction, her shoulder pressed against his, Bridget at his father's birthday party playing horseshoes with his arms around her. Her silky hair, her sizzling kisses. He buried his head in his hands and asked himself what was more risky, to stick to the status quo or to take a chance on happiness so sublime he had to keep pushing it to the back of his mind for fear of doing something crazy.

He was hard-pressed to answer the inevitable questions from everyone he saw. There was Max's plaintive, "Why, Dad, *why* did she have to leave?"

There was, "How's Bridget?" from his mother, accompanied with a knowing look.

There was, "Whaddya hear from Bridget?" from his old classmates.

He couldn't go to town without someone stopping him to ask about her. What could he say? I haven't heard from her, and I'm not going to? No, all he could do was to mumble something about she was fine but very busy and so forth. But how did he know she was fine or that she was busy? He could have called her, of course. He still had the card she'd given him that first day, but he had no excuse for calling. If she was interested in him, she would have called him.

But there was no call, no message on his answering machine. She was no doubt swept up in the ad campaign for the cologne, or maybe she'd moved on to a new account. She was back to her former life, a life that made Harmony look dull. Maybe she was out looking for another symbol, right now, today, as he repaired the fence on his upper pasture in an futile effort to get his mind off Bridget and onto more practical matters.

Instead, he stood there, with the roll of fence wire lying on the ground, imagining that this time Bridget was looking for a man who looked good in running shoes or who ate cold cereal for breakfast. The idea of her photographing some other guy, a guy who had no five-year-old son, who'd never suffered a heart-breaking loss, who came with no baggage, who was available for a long-term commitment, caused him to grind his teeth in frustration.

Because this man, whoever he was, would be powerless to resist Bridget's quirky charm. He'd be bowled over by her honesty, her determination and her kindness. Not to mention those meltingly soft eyes, her determined chin, her kissable lips. And he would be sweeping her off her feet with flattery, plying her with promises. And she would listen, she'd believe, because she was so vulnerable, so lovable, that he himself had fallen in love with her!

In love with Bridget? He couldn't be. And yet what other reason could there be for the way he felt? For the way she'd turned his life upside down? For the way she'd come and taken up residence in his heart? He hit his forehead with his fist.

Maybe he should have tried to sweep her off her feet with compliments. If anything he'd been too honest, about his problems and about his past. He'd scared her away by unloading his whole psyche on her that last night. He'd seen the look in her eyes even by moonlight, he saw how he'd overwhelmed her with his sad story. What woman wants to hear the sad story of your life? No one. Especially not Bridget.

She'd gone back to her other life just as fast as she could. It was too late to impress her, to win her over. He had no idea how to do that. He and Molly had gotten married because they'd always been in love and were sure they always would be. It was so easy. Now he was out of step. Out of tune. It was over...unless...unless... He picked up his fence wire, hooked it to his saddle and rode back to the ranch. The fencing could wait.

That night, after Max had fallen asleep, after he'd asked for the hundredth time when Bridget was coming back, Josh went to the living room and took Molly's high school graduation picture off the mantel. He held it by the frame between his thumb and forefinger, looking at her innocent, youthful face, gazing into her warm brown eyes.

"Molly," he said. "I don't know how to tell you this. Maybe you already know. I've fallen in love with someone else. I didn't think it was possible, but it is. It took me off guard. I fought it off because I was so scared. Scared of loving and losing," he said, leaning against the back of an upholstered arm chair. "I want you to know that I'll always treasure the love we shared. I can't remember a time when I didn't love you, when I didn't know that someday I'd marry you. It might have been in fifth grade, or maybe even sooner. We grew up together, and I thought, I believed, I'd never love again after you died, but Bridget came along, and I realized there was something missing from my life. And from Max's life."

He paused and imagined that Molly's sweet smile deepened. Maybe it was wishful thinking, but he suddenly felt that she understood, that she really did want him to be happy. That she wanted him to take another chance on happiness.

"I miss you, Molly," he said, his throat tightening over a lump the size of a horseshoe. "You were such an important part of my life. You were my rock. My center of gravity. No one will every replace you. No one could ever take your place," he continued, running a finger over the outline of her face.

Her eyes looked back at him, warm and kind and encouraging. And he knew without a doubt that she only wanted his happiness. His and Max's. Now and forever. He knew, too, that happiness was within his grasp. If he would only take that chance.

"I don't know how Bridget feels," he said. "But I wanted, I needed to talk to you before I did anything. I had to let you know." He pressed the framed picture against his forehead for a long moment and he realized that the glass, instead of cold and hard as it was a moment ago, was now warm to the touch.

"Thank you, Molly," he whispered. Then he took the picture and carefully wrapped it in one of the small yellow hand towels they'd gotten for their wedding, and put it in a wooden box on the shelf in his closet next to Molly's jewelry box.

The Wild Mustang men's cologne launch party was a huge success. The first floor of Macy's department store on the corner of Geary and Stockton Streets was packed with women lined up to buy the highly touted fragrance for the men in their lives, and with men wanting to buy it for themselves. There was a country and western band playing on the mezzanine. Even Bridget's ex-fiancé, Scott, was there, looking and sounding suitably impressed, both with the cologne and with her.

"What have you done to yourself, Bridget?" he asked, his gaze sweeping over the hat and the leather boots she'd purchased at the dry goods store in Harmony. "You look terrific. This Western motif suits you."

"Does it?" How was it she never noticed how cool he was, how effete and how superficial? Or was he just an average, normal city man who paled in contrast with the honest, earthy, sexy rancher she couldn't get out of her mind?

"You've done a fantastic job with this cologne thing, you know. Tell me—" Scott motioned to the picture of

Josh on the wall. "Is this guy for real? Or is he a computerized image?"

"He's real." Very real. The most real person she'd ever known. Her gaze veered to one of the huge colored posters of Josh on his horse silhouetted against the western sunset. She had to admit it was a spectacular shot. It conveyed everything she'd hoped it would. Strength, virility, power and sex appeal—all that and more. Even after all these weeks, she couldn't look at it without feeling a surge of heart-wrenching loss.

"It must be lonely out there, in business for yourself," Scott said. "Come back, Bridget. We can work together again. I know we can. I've missed you." He gave her his most charming smile, and she felt a cold chill go up her spine.

"Not a chance," she said, matching his smile with one just as phony as his.

"Well, no harm in asking," he said. Then he kissed her on the lips and drifted away.

Bridget wiped his kiss off her lips with the back of her hand. Lonely? She'd never known the meaning of the word until she came back from Harmony. But it had nothing to do with being in business for herself, and it had everything to do with missing Josh. Every minute of every day. No matter that she'd been busier than she'd ever been in her life. Kate told her it would take time to get over him. She'd known that. She just hadn't known how painful it would be.

From where she stood on a riser she could see the main entrance to the store. Though she kept it in her line of sight, she wasn't looking for Josh. She wasn't waiting for him to come through the door. She knew he wouldn't come, though she'd sent him an invitation with a check for the work he'd done. Then who was she looking for? Nobody. She didn't know. She only knew there was a knot in her stomach just under her rib cage that had been lodged there since early morning and that nothing could unravel—not even an offer to go back to her old agency.

It shouldn't be surprising that she felt nervous. This was a big event. She'd planned it, she'd worked on it for months, and she was responsible for its success. Of course she was jumpy. The client had wanted Josh to be there in person, dressed in his checkered shirt, his vest and his well-worn Levi's as he was in his picture. Bridget told them it was impossible. He was busy. He was tied up. They didn't have to know he was violently against men's cologne—wouldn't buy it, wouldn't wear it, wouldn't promote it any more than he'd already done, wouldn't even smell it. Especially if it smelled like wild mustangs. And certainly wouldn't come to an event celebrating it. Especially if he knew Bridget would be there.

She'd never forget that last night, and she knew he wouldn't, either. The way he'd held her at arm's length after confiding in her was symbolic of how he was going to keep her at a distance for now and forever. He'd probably forgotten about her already, while she thought about him every minute of every day. That was understandable. She'd been working on promoting this cologne nonstop since her return from Harmony. After tonight she could forget about men's cologne and Josh and Max and start on a new account. She was in demand now, and there were several possibilities.

One possibility was a new facial tissue. Another was nonalcoholic beer. Strange how they didn't excite her the way wild mustangs did. Face it, nothing excited her the way wild mustangs did, except the man who trained them. She rubbed her hand across her forehead and leaned back against the kiosk at the edge of the men's department. She'd get excited tomorrow, after this was over. She was just tired, that was all. Tired of the rat race. Tired of the traffic and the noise on the street and the constantly ringing telephones inside her office.

She'd take a rest before she decided which account to take on next. Get away from it all. Her mind drifted back to the most get-away-from-it-all place she'd ever been. To its clean fresh air. To the friendly people who'd opened their hearts and their homes to her. To a little boy whose little freckled face would forever haunt her memory as would his voice, saying, "If my dad finds out, he'll have my hide." It seemed like yesterday that he'd come out of nowhere, crashing into her on his bicycle.

Bridget had stood there so long, staring at the giant poster of Josh on his horse, she was beginning to hallucinate. As the band played "Stand by Your Man" she imagined she saw him in the middle of the crowd, not in his checkered shirt and well-worn Levi's, but in a blue chambray shirt, a dark tie and khaki pants and brown leather Top-Siders. That's how she knew he was a mirage.

The Josh Gentry she knew didn't wear a tie. Or anything on his feet but boots. Yet there was something about the way he walked, the way he shaded his eyes from the bright lights, the way his hair fell over her forehead that made her blood race, her heart pound and her mouth go dry as Nevada dust.

She couldn't move. She just stood there watching him. When he saw her, he dropped his arm to his side, and their eyes met and held for a long moment. Before she knew what she was doing, she was pushing her way through the crowd, her heart in her throat, fearing she might lose him in the masses of customers desperate to buy an ounce of cologne. Why was he here? Why had he changed his mind and decided to come to the launch? Why, why, why?

Breathless, panting and pink-cheeked she finally ran into him somewhere near the accessories counter. Really ran into him, hard enough to feel muscles in his chest, the heat from his body, to smell the crisp clean smell of all outdoors, of horses and leather and most of all of him—the man she'd missed so much there was an heavy ache in her heart that threatened her ability to speak or think.

Instantly she backed away from him as if she'd been burned and gripped the edge of a nearby counter to keep from falling on the floor or blurting something stupid like she was glad to see him. She forced her lips into the semblance of a smile.

"This is a surprise," she said, proud of how steady her voice was. "I didn't expect you."

"I didn't expect to come," he said, his hands on his hips, his eyes probing, searching, asking questions she couldn't answer.

"Why did you?" she asked. She had to know. She couldn't allow herself to hope, to believe, to imagine....

He looked around the room at the crowds, the lights, the band, the posters. The muscles in his jaw tensed and then forcibly relaxed before he spoke. "I had to see for myself. What your life was all about. What it was you wanted. What drove you. Now I know. Congratulations."

"Thank you. But this isn't all of my life." She gestured to the hot-air balloons in desert colors and the acres of people still milling around. "I do have a personal life, too."

He smiled grimly. "I'll bet you do."

"I'm finished here. Come home with me. See my place."

"I don't think so."

"You're not going back tonight, are you?" she asked.

"No, but—"

"Spend the night on my couch. I owe you." She tried to sound casual and not as desperate as she felt. If he said no, she'd throw herself at him, beg him, plead with him, follow him home if need be.

He looked like she'd asked him to let her take target

practice with him as the target. "I'm not spending the night on your couch," he said.

"At least come for coffee. I-I've missed you."

He shrugged, and before he could say no, she was trying to keep up with his long-legged stride as he walked out of the store and up the street to the Sutter-Stockton garage where he'd left his truck. Fortunately she'd left her car at home and come by taxi, because she was terrified that if she let him out of her sight, he'd disappear from her life forever. He might do that, anyway, but she was going to do her damnedest to keep that from happening.

She sat next to him in the passenger seat of his truck, her hands holding on to the edge of the seat for the white-knuckle ride to her Russian Hill apartment. He drove fast, expertly, up and over the steep hills as if he'd lived there all his life. He didn't speak, he just turned where she said to turn and parked in the garage under her building.

The apartment seemed smaller than ever with him there. He filled the living room with his presence, overwhelmed the leather furniture, the lamps and the carpets—and especially, her.

"I've got to get out of these clothes," she said, tossing the felt hat onto her desk and kicking off her boots. "I feel ridiculous. Here I am in Western clothes, while you look like you belong here."

"But I don't," he said

"I know that," she said, taking a step toward her bedroom so she could change.

"Any more than you belong on a ranch in Nevada." His voice was a low monotone.

She whirled around. His features were cast in stone. Like the words he said.

What could she possibly say to show him, to tell him, to ask him— "You mean because I wasn't born there, is that it?"

"Because you belong here," he said, with a glance out the window at the sparkling lights of the city and the Bay Bridge in the distance. "Because you want what this life can give you...*has* given you. Don't tell me you don't want it. I saw you tonight. I saw you the people congratulate you, the man who kissed you. I heard the music, I saw the band. I can't compete with that."

She stared at him in disbelief. "You think I want that? You think that means anything to me?"

"You told me it did."

"I know I did," she admitted, walking back into the living room. "Yes, I told you I wanted success. I couldn't tell you I wanted love even more. You would have pitied me. I couldn't tell anyone how much, all these years, I've wanted a husband, a house and a baby. Of course I needed money. I had no one to support me, and I had to prove it to myself and to everyone who didn't believe in me that I could do it. Well, I did it. And now I want what I've always wanted more than anything. If I hadn't come to Harmony I never would have known you. I might have gone on for years in this world, from ad campaign to ad campaign. But my life wouldn't have been complete. There would have been a void in it ten feet wide. Because I never knew what it was like to belong to a place, a community, a family like yours." She stopped and licked her dry lips.

"Not that I belong there...not that I'd ever belong there the way you do...." Oh, God, she was going to break down, to start crying before she'd even said what she wanted to say.

"So what are you going to do?" he asked. "Come back and set up shop on Main Street? How long do you think you'd last? No challenge, no business, no view, no adulation?"

"Would you stop that?" she demanded hotly. "I told you I've done what I set out to do, to prove I could make it on my own. Yes, I'm a success. Yes, I'm proud of myself. But I don't need people telling me I'm wonderful every day. I just need...I just need—'' She choked on the word she couldn't say. The hot tears gushed down her face. She turned and ran to her room, not caring if he left in disgust or not. She had swallowed every bit of pride she'd ever had. She'd come as close as she could to confessing she loved him, to begging him to take her back to Harmony with him. And there he stood, stony-faced and unfeeling. Now it was up to him.

She slammed the door behind her and threw herself on her bed, crying such anguished sobs that she didn't hear him throw her door open.

She was only vaguely aware of his footsteps crossing the room, of him sitting on the edge of her bed, of his hands on her shoulders, soothing, calming, massaging gently. ''What is it you need, Bridget?'' he asked, when her sobs had died down to a mere torrent instead of a flood. ''Tell me and I'll get it for you.''

He wiped the tears from her cheek with the pad of his thumb, and she started in again. This time so touched by his tenderness she was unable to stop crying. He stretched out next to her on her blue-and-white handmade quilt, facing her across the pattern of hearts and flowers.

''Please stop crying,'' he said, tracing his broad callused finger around her cheek.

She nodded and swallowed hard. ''I'm all right now.''

''Sure?''

She heaved a shaky sigh and nodded.

He dug his elbow into her quilt, propped his head on his palm and looked at her. His expression had softened, a hint of a smile tugged at one corner of his mouth. His eyes were no longer ice-blue; they flickered with pinpoints of light. ''You still haven't told me what you need,'' he prodded.

She hesitated. What did she have to lose? Just Josh and Max and her whole future, that was all.

"I need *you*," she said so softly he would have missed it if he hadn't leaned forward, if his lips hadn't been so close he could feel the words as she formed them.

He put his arms around her then and crushed her to him until she felt his heart beating in time to her own.

"Are you sure you can give up everything else?" he muttered in her ear. "All the things you've worked for. This view, this—"

"This noise, this stress, this pressure, this city. This is nothing compared to…"

"To what…Harmony? Would you really consider living with me, with *us*, on the ranch?" Josh asked, rolling over so she was lying on top of him, her breasts cushioned against his chest, her hips pressed invitingly against his, her full lips only a breath away from his.

He thought he knew the answer to his question. But she didn't speak. She just lay there looking at him, her expression dazed, her eyes glazed with disbelief.

"Are you sure, sure you're ready to take a chance with me?" she asked anxiously.

"Sure. Very sure. I tried to ignore you. I tried to pretend I didn't love you. I tried to put you out of my life and out of my mind and out of my heart. But you refused to budge. Molly will always be a part of my past. But you, you're my present and my future. My life. Say yes, would you?" he demanded. "Would you just say yes? Because my heart has stopped beating, and my watch has stopped running. Nothing works without you. I need you, Bridget, don't you see that? And I love you. More than anything."

She exhaled lightly, and her smile lit her face. "I love you, too," she breathed. "So the answer is yes, I'll consider it."

She twined her arms around his neck and kissed him

then, hungrily and deeply, showing him better than words, how seriously she would consider living with him forever and ever.

"Another thing," he said, coming up for air, minutes or maybe hours later. "Would you consider taking on the public relations for the Wild Mustang Association? It's time for the world to know about them."

"As long as I have time for my bike riding and slingshot lessons," she said, nuzzling her face against his neck.

He grinned. "I want to tell somebody. I want to tell the world about us. Tell them how much I love you."

"You mean you're going to put it in the *Harmony Times?*" she asked.

"I mean I'm going to shout it out the window, right now."

"Josh," she said, sitting on the edge of the bed, wide-eyed, her hair tousled, her eyes glowing, her heart spilling over with love. "You wouldn't."

He stuck his head out the open window. "I'm in love with Bridget McCloud," he said into the night air. "And she's in love with me."

Bridget jumped up and joined him at the window. Horns honked, sirens shrieked and lights went on and off as the whole city seemed to celebrate their love. Bridget sighed happily and closed the window.

"Wait a minute," he said, taking her by the shoulders. "I forgot to tell the world you're going to marry me. You are, aren't you?"

Smiling, she nodded, deliriously, ridiculously happy. "The sooner the better."

"And we're going to give Max the brothers and sisters he needs to keep him from becoming a spoiled only child?"

"Absolutely," she said loosening his tie and tugging him

toward her until his face was so close she could see into the depths of his eyes and his mouth was just a kiss away from hers. ''The sooner the better.''

* * * * *

Take 2 bestselling love stories FREE

Plus get a FREE surprise gift!

International bestselling author

JOAN JOHNSTON

continues her wildly popular Hawk's Way
miniseries with an all-new, longer-length novel

THE SUBSTITUTE GROOM

HAWK'S WAY

August 1998

Jennifer Wright's hopes and dreams had rested on her summer wedding—until a single moment changed everything. Including the *groom*. Suddenly Jennifer agreed to marry her fiancé's best friend, a darkly handsome Texan she needed—and desperately wanted—almost against her will. But U.S. Air Force Major Colt Whitelaw had sacrificed too much to settle for a marriage of convenience, and that made hiding her passion all the more difficult. And hiding her biggest secret downright impossible...

"Joan Johnston does contemporary Westerns to perfection." *—Publishers Weekly*

Available in August 1998
wherever Silhouette books are sold.

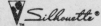

Look us up on-line at: http://www.romance.net   PSHWKWAY

In **July 1998** comes

THE
MACKENZIE
FAMILY

by *New York Times* bestselling author

LINDA
HOWARD

The dynasty continues with:

Mackenzie's Pleasure: Rescuing a pampered ambassador's daughter from her terrorist kidnappers was a piece of cake for navy SEAL Zane Mackenzie. It was only afterward, when they were alone together, that the real danger began....

Mackenzie's Magic: Talented trainer Maris Mackenzie was wanted for horse theft, but with no memory, she had little chance of proving her innocence or eluding the real villains. Her only hope for salvation? The stranger in her bed.

Available this July for the first time ever in a two-in-one trade-size edition. Fall in love with the Mackenzies for the first time—or all over again!

Available at your favorite retail outlet.

Silhouette Books